Demon Hunters

The Black Knight

Dark-Age evil rises.
Witchcraft & sorcery plague the realm.
Guinevere is missing. Arthur is at war.
Hope is a knight in black.

Camelot's greatest champion must
return to save Albion's queen.

Demon Hunters

Heroic Fantasy through the Ages

Books by Iestyn Long

The Timothy Williams Saga

Book One: Demon Hunter
Book Two: The Infernal Shadow

Demon Hunters

The Black Knight
The Chronicles of Cassius
Zen Lee & The Yellow Emperor

Other Stories

Merry Christmas and a Happy End of the World

Demon Hunters
The Black Knight

By Iestyn Long

Copyright © 2021-2023 Iestyn Long

Arthur's website: https://www.demon-hunter.co.uk
E-Store: https://www.demonhuntersupplies.co.uk

ISBN: 978-1-9160177-5-7

Chapter One

The Great Wrym

The scent of death filled the Black Knight's nostrils. Evil was afoot.

The knight held a burning brand aloft, the flame spluttering in the dark, fetid air, casting sinister shapes upon the walls of earth and rock. He gripped the hilt of a sword in his other hand, the honed blade glinting in the firelight.

Halting, he listened…

There was nothing but the sound of his laboured breath and the whooshing and popping of the flaming torch.

Using the crossguard of his sword, he pushed open his visor. *Should the air beneath the ground not be cool?* In these cursed tunnels, it was stifling.

The knight descended. Soon, a growing stench accompanied his journey, a repugnant aroma threatening to overwhelm his senses. The further he crept into the waiting darkness, the fouler his environment became.

How far underground am I? He had stalked the creature's rank-smelling subterranean world deeper and deeper but had yet to encounter the monstrosity lurking within. *Where are you, foul slug?*

Beneath the world of men, the Black Knight ventured ever lower. The size of his ungodly foe was no mystery, not when the passageways he walked were evidently created by the monster itself. Negotiating the way ahead was simple enough. He had no need to bend his back or dip his head. *What manner of thing can tunnel through earth and rock?*

The route widened, and although the flickering torchlight revealed little of his whereabouts, the knight realised he had emerged into an open space. The air was cooler here, and the rushing of a waterfall could be heard amidst the darkness.

The great wyrm's lair. Seemingly, the creature had burrowed into an underground cavern.

The knight ventured into the unknown, his booted feet crunching with each step. Lowering his torch, he illuminated a grim carpet of bones littering the soil. *The remnants of the monster's victims.*

The Black Knight offered a silent prayer for the souls of the dead, vowing to bring the creature and its cruel-hearted mistress to justice. *This is Morgana's doing*, he thought grimly. Torn from the perpetual darkness of the Otherworld, the witch had unleashed the demon upon the world above.

And now it is time to return the monster from whence it came.

Retracing his steps, the Black Knight positioned himself at the head of the tunnel. He had no wish to grant the fearsome thing space in which to manoeuvre.

'Awake, wyrm!' the knight cried, his voice echoing through the vast emptiness of the cavern.

Nothing stirred in the gloom.

'Awake, I say!'

The Black Knight waited, yet only the distant roar of the tumbling waterfall answered his call. 'I know you linger here. Your foul scent betrays your presence. Show yourself!'

At first, he felt a tremor, and then the ground on which the knight stood began to shake. In moments, he was rocking back and forth as if floundering aboard a ship's deck amid a violent storm. Suddenly, the earth below his feet fell away, plunging into nothingness. The knight scrambled into the passageway, seeking solid ground. A gaping hole yawned where once he stood, and from its black depths rose the Great Wyrm of Corbyn.

Lit by the knight's flashing flame, the ghastly beast reared high above him—an immense pulsating worm, its hide an oozing mass of pale flesh swathed with foot-long barbs, each dripping with toxic slime, its eyeless head a grotesque misshapen lump protected by an army of jutting tusks and horns—the beast's terrible tools for dismantling earth and rock and dissecting flesh and bone. And at the centre of the wyrm's hideous head was a monstrous maw thrice lined with cruel black teeth—an unholy abyss leading straight to Hell, and from this dark orifice issued the odour of death.

The wyrm recoiled, its immense bulk twisting from the light. The demon plunged headlong into the tunnel toward its foe, seeking to extinguish the source of its misery.

The Black Knight thrust his torch at the gruesome monster and swung his sword, slicing the blade deep into its noxious flesh.

Screeching, the wyrm retreated a second time.

The knight fled. But soon, the awful beast returned. *I must face the demon or else be consumed by it.*

The knight turned. Again, he held the flame aloft. Yet this time, driven by a terrible rage, the wyrm was undeterred by the light and surged hungrily at its prey, mouth wide open.

The Black Knight threw himself aside. The torch in his hand spluttered, its orange flame dancing wildly, projecting the horrifying scene like a puppet show upon the walls. The beast's huge bulbous head swung to smash him against the rock. The knight swayed aside from the blow, and after another slash of his sword, he was gone.

The great slug followed, propelling its undulating length through the underground shaft. Swiftly, the creature was atop its foe once more.

The knight spun and, with lightning speed, slipped inside the monster's deadly horns and tusks to deliver yet another wound to its glutinous head. An ear-piercing screech resonated in the dark.

I must entice the slug above ground to even the odds. Making a stand here was folly. The Black Knight lured it higher, each bite of his snaking blade driving the wyrm mad with fury, baiting the beast from its lair. The pair fought a running battle, climbing toward the surface through the creature's twisting subterranean burrow.

Only a little further. The Black Knight cut and ran, cut and ran—again and again. The monster chased. Then blackness… the knight's torch extinguished. He strove on regardless, scrabbling desperately in the dark, the beast's piercing shriek and toxic breath—enough to subdue lesser men—ever nearer.

There is light ahead.

Straining every muscle within his beleaguered body, the Black Knight launched himself free of the tunnel. The great wyrm pursued him, bursting from the ground into the world above. At once, it screamed in torment, its sensitive hide blistering beneath the midday sun.

In the monster's moment of misery, the Black Knight struck. Braving the tusks and teeth, he drove his blade deep inside the demon's cavernous maw, ramming the cold metal of his weapon through the roof of its mouth and into its brain. The Great Wyrm of Corbyn—the bane of King Pelles and his people—was dead.

Joy erupted. The folk of Corbyn crowded the Black Knight, proclaiming him their saviour. They praised him, embraced him, kissed him, marvelling at his heroic deed.

'Your victory, good sir knight, is worthy of any told,' King Pelles acclaimed.

The Black Knight did not answer. Warm wetness seeped between his skin and armour from underneath his right arm. He was bleeding. *A cursed tusk or tooth has punctured my mail.* He began to feel strange. A cold weariness clouded his thoughts and numbed his limbs.

'Sir knight?'

The Black Knight's vision swam. An icy chill gripped his heart. The cheering crowds became like the roaring of the sea, deafening and despairing. He took a trembling step toward King Pelles... and fell into darkness.

Chapter Two

May-Day

The queen urged her dappled grey mare into the water. Lifting her hooves high, the noble steed splashed eagerly across the ford before mounting the shallow bank opposite.

'Good girl,' Guinevere praised. Leaning forward in the saddle, she patted the animal's neck. 'Come, Meredith, let us feel the wind in our hair.'

Guinevere kicked her mount into a canter and pounded into the wide expanse of lush wild meadow stretching into the distance.

'This is the place,' Guinevere yelled into the onrushing wind.

Queen and horse raced through a swaying sea of tall grass and vibrant blooms alive with bees and birds. It was a joy to be amongst nature and its wonders. To feel the sun on her face and fresh air in her lungs, to be free from the dreary confines of Camelot, was a blessing. Guinevere cherished every moment.

After a brief but exhilarating ride, Guinevere pulled on the reins and slowed Meredith to a walk. The queen meandered, enjoying the solitude and the glorious scene encircling her.

'This is perfect,' she whispered. But, of course, she already knew that it was. She had been here before. The fresh green of new spring leaves coloured the western horizon, an ancient woodland of oak and ash as old as Albion herself. To the east, the gentle waters of the River Camlann coiled through the countryside like a giant silver serpent. And between wood and river, the flowering meadow sprang wild and beautiful.

The white spires of Camelot shimmered in the distance. *Only a league from here,* Guinevere mused. *Yet it is so remote and peaceful here I could be a hundred leagues away.*

'A splendid choice, my Queen,' Sir Ladinas proclaimed, leading the queen's entourage across the meadow to join her. 'Seldom have I seen a prettier spot.'

Guinevere smiled. 'Come then, good sir knights, what do you wait for? The sun is shining, and the birds are singing. Choose your ladies, and we shall ride a-maying.'

The queen's attendants prepared a feast upon the meadow, and while the servants bent to their task, Guinevere and her joyous party set forth. Dressed in green and sharing their mounts with maidens, the knights rode through the tall grass and vibrant blooms into the nearby woods, where they began harvesting a bounty of flowers and herbs.

The arrival of spring had not always been so well celebrated. In the dark days before King Arthur's reign and in the years of turmoil following his succession, when peace was only a dream and war ravaged all the land, it was not so.

Eventually, Arthur won his peace. But as always, war lingers with intent, forever lurking on the horizon. Evil, it seems, never sleeps. And even as the queen revisited an old custom and celebrated the promise of fairer days to come, her king and his knights were abroad in the east protecting Albion and Arthur's brave new world against the endless Saxon scourge. Yet, it is the demons in the dark that kings and queens must watch for.

The morning passed, and with flushed cheeks and smiling faces, the knights and their maidens returned from the far reaches of the glorious meadow. The feast was set, and while Guinevere's minstrels played many a fine tune, the ladies weaved garlands fashioned from the beautiful blooms and fragrant flowers they had so lovingly gathered amongst the trees and fields.

Guinevere beamed. To see so many of Camelot's young knights paired with the beautiful maidens of the court filled her heart with joy. 'And all blessed beneath spring sunshine,' she whispered contentedly. She realised the day's success was but a small thing. Yet life at court was seldom anything other than tedious, especially without Arthur, and dare she think it, without Sir Lancelot du Lac. Guinevere's heart was heavy in their absence.

Laughing and giggling, the maidens crowned their knights with their creations, and the minstrels played on. Mirth and merriment were enjoyed by one and all. At noon, the May Day feast began, and upon a white cloth, the queen's attendants brought forth platters of venison and roasted fowl, loaves of bread, and flagons of wine. While the party ate and drank their fill, the minstrels recounted them with yarns—rousing tales of heroism for the proud studs and heartfelt stories of lost love for the young fillies.

During a recital of the tragic tale of Tristan and Isolde, Guinevere's eyes were drawn to the green wood, and her thoughts wistfully wandered to a time shared amidst the trees and beneath the leaves with Camelot's lost champion. *Alas, those times are gone.* Not since the winter solstice—five years past—had Sir Lancelot graced Camelot with his presence nor anywhere else in Albion. The king was much aggrieved by Sir Lancelot's disappearance. He was Arthur's champion but also his friend, their bond as strong as brothers. *Yet none miss him more than I.*

There was no suggestion that Arthur suspected infidelity. Why should he? The very notion was unthinkable. Guilt gnawed at Guinevere's soul, but she could not change the past. What was done was done. All she could do now was make amends by being a good queen for both Arthur and Albion. *A queen must do her duty just as a king must.*

As Tristan and Isolde's story came to its sad end, a glint of light cast from the treeline caught Guinevere's attention. 'Tell me, Sir Kay, what is that glare beside the wood?'

Sir Kay stood before squinting into the distance. 'I know not, my Queen.'

Sir Agravain and Sir Sagramour lent their keen eyes to the task.

'I believe it is a knight, my Queen,' Sir Sagramour said, shielding the sun from his eyes with a cupped hand. 'Or at least a soldier. See how the sunlight reflects from his armour? And beneath him, a horse, do you not think?'

'Yes, I see now.' For a fleeting, fanciful moment, Guinevere hoped the knight was Sir Lancelot returning to her. Yet the knight was promptly joined by a force of fighting men who, like woodland sprites, appeared from the trees sparkling silver beneath the sun.

'A host approaches,' Sir Sagramour announced. 'With your leave, my Queen, permit me to ride and meet with them.'

'It is wise council,' Sir Kay advised. 'These knights fly no banner, nor do they display their lord's crest upon shield or surcoat. Not that I can tell, at any rate.' The distance between themselves and their unexpected visitors was too great to be sure of anything. Yet their presence unsettled the knight.

Sir Sagramour mounted his stallion. 'I will parley with them, and perhaps we shall learn something of their purpose.'

'You have my gratitude, sir,' Guinevere acknowledged. 'And meanwhile, we shall prepare to leave this place and return to Camelot.' Like Sir Kay, she was surprised by the unannounced arrival of the soldiers.

The queen's attendants began to pack away the remnants of the feast, and all the while, the young knights and their ladies observed the advancing troops with curiosity. They saw Sir Sagramour well-met by a giant of a man mounted atop a huge black charger. Soon, Sir Sagramour was riding at the stranger's side, and all seemed well.

Four and forty strong, the unknown host crossed the green meadow, crushing the tall grass and vibrant blooms beneath their booted feet. Arriving at last before the queen and her party, Sir Sagramour edged his mount toward Guinevere, and the giant knight followed. 'My Queen, I have the honour of introducing Sir Tarquin of Tallyhorn.'

The knight in question tilted his fearsome bull-horned helmet, but neither did he speak nor open his visor as all well-mannered knights ought in the company of a lady, not least a queen.

'Sir Tarquin?' Guinevere pondered. 'Your name is familiar, sir knight.'

Suddenly, swords sang into the air. Sir Kay and Sir Agravain had drawn their blades. 'Treachery, my Queen!' Sir Kay cried. 'This man is a tyrant! Since Arthur's ascension, Sir Tarquin and his master have held a grudge.'

'How so?' Inwardly, Guinevere was shocked by the actions of her knights, and her heart began racing faster and faster. What was this knight doing here, and what were his intentions? The man filled her with dread. His bull-helmeted head was demon-like, and his bearing fearsome. She hoped her growing apprehension did not show.

'The craven knight covets lands not his own. And more than that, all know of his desire to do Sir Lancelot wrong after our champion slew his brother in combat.'

Sir Agravain hawked and spat. 'He is nothing but a robber knight, my Queen, and his ill deeds precede him.'

'I see Camelot's welcome is as warm as winter,' Sir Tarquin stated, his voice gruff like a wolf's growl.

'I care not for welcomes,' Sir Agravain countered. 'Do you deny these charges against you?'

Sir Tarquin snorted. 'I do. My lands are mine by right, and Sir Lancelot du Lac is a murderer. When I find him, I will kill him. As for the crimes I am about to commit, well, that is a different matter.'

'Treasonous talk, sir!' the queen answered angrily. She turned to Sir Sagramour for answers. 'What is the meaning of this? Explain yourself?'

Sir Sagramour smiled apologetically. 'Alas, I cannot. Needless to say, I will be considerably wealthier by sundown.'

'Traitor!' Sir Agravain roared, shielding the queen with his body. 'You will answer for your deceit!'

Sir Tarquin and Sir Sagramour wheeled their steeds away. 'Seize the queen,' Sir Tarquin commanded his men. 'Kill the others!'

At once, Sir Tarquin's soldiers levelled their spears.

Brandishing their swords, the young knights of Camelot assembled beside Sir Kay and Sir Agravain, sheltering the queen and her entourage behind them.

'You are brazen indeed, sir robber knight, to conduct your villainy within plain sight of my husband's stronghold,'

Guinevere accused, desperately trying to tame her trembling voice. 'And think not that my knights will be easy prey, even unarmoured as they are. They are knights of Camelot, and Sir Kay and Sir Agravain are knights of the Round Table!'

Sir Tarquin mocked Guinevere, 'It matters not how good your pretty green knights are, my little queen. When they face spear and sword without mail and shield, they will quickly find themselves butchered like pigs at slaughter.'

The ground shook with pounding hoofbeats. The sounds of music and merriment were usurped by the cries and screams of battle. Sir Tarquin's men thundered into Sir Kay and his defenders, and without spears and shields to brace against the charge, the mounted men tore through Camelot's knights, scattering them like May blossom caught in the throes of a winter storm. The queen's ladies and attendants fled, shrieking into the meadow, their flushed cheeks streaked with salty tears and their thumping hearts heavy with woe.

Sir Kay hacked a thrusting spear aside, and as the rider powered past him atop a chestnut steed, he lashed him with his sword, sweeping him from his saddle.

Sir Agravain, ever a knight of valour and possessing a heart as stout as any knight to have lived, refused to yield ground to man or beast. As his opponent was all but on him, Sir Agravain plunged his blade into the knight's mount, sending both horse and rider crashing into a writhing heap.

'Protect the queen!' Sir Kay bellowed.

Many of Camelot's young knights pursued their ladies across the meadow, hoping to catch and defend them against the robber knights. These gallant yet foolhardy men were ruthlessly cut down by Sir Tarquin's mounted soldiers, and their ladies hauled, kicking and screaming, over the enemy's saddles or slain with blade or spear to join their menfolk amidst the grass.

Sir Kay and Sir Agravain, supported by those knights wise enough not to break from the pack, fought a stout rear guard. But cut by cut, Camelot's brave warriors began to waver. Wounded in many places, their green May Day livery was stained red with blood. Yet they fought on, prepared to defend their queen until their last breath.

Beyond the battle's perimeter, Sir Tarquin and Sir Sagramour watched proceedings from their saddles. 'Your friends fight well, Sir Sagramour,' Sir Tarquin observed. 'Too well.' The giant knight was unimpressed meeting with such resistance, especially when he had been assured there would be none. 'I think it is time you lent my men your sword.'

Confused, Sir Sagramour twisted in his saddle to face Sir Tarquin. 'What of our agreement, sir?'

'Enter the fray, Sir Sagramour,' Sir Tarquin insisted, slapping the rump of the traitorous knight's horse with the flat of his blade.

Sir Sagramour's steed bore him into the thick of battle and clad in May Day greenery, the turncoat was quickly spotted by Camelot's knights.

'Behold, the renegade knight!' Sir Agravain bellowed. In a maddened rage, the veteran charged at Sir Sagramour, slaying all in his path and taking many wounds for his troubles. Once Sir Agravain faced the traitor, he cleaved the spineless knight from his horse and, with a mighty blow, separated his head from his body.

Sir Tarquin had seen enough. Kicking his warhorse into action, the giant knight circled the battle, searching for a weakness he might exploit. 'There!' To Guinevere's rear, Camelot's knights had been drawn into the melee, leaving her defences thin. The giant spurred his mount into the breach and rode directly for the queen. 'Onward!'

Sir Osanna barred Sir Tarquin's way. The giant knight lent low in his saddle and slashed down with his sword, opening Sir Osanna's throat. Next, charging from the melee, Sir Tillius hammered into Sir Tarquin's flank. Both riders and their mounts crashed to the earth. Amidst the animals' flailing hooves, it was a race between the two men to regain their senses and footing. Unscathed, the giant rose first, and brave Sir Tillius fell to the robber knight's wrath.

Either engaged or fallen in battle, Camelot's knights could not help Sir Ladinas, for he alone stood between Sir Tarquin and his prize.

'For the queen!'

Beneath the bright May sun, the young knight surged through the meadow like a prowling wolf, and the formidable Sir Tarquin was his prey.

'Insolent pup!'

Sir Ladinas was swept aside as if he were nothing more than a child. Then, as the wounded warrior struggled to rise, the giant knight swung his weapon, smashing him into the ground for good.

Sir Tarquin's gaze fell upon Camelot's queen.

Guinevere reached into the long grass, arming herself with Sir Ladinas' fallen sword. 'Come no closer!' she screamed, swishing the blade through the warm spring air. 'I warn you, knave, I am well versed in the use of sword, axe and spear.'

Sir Tarquin snorted. 'I do not doubt it,' he said, edging closer. 'But why not prevent further losses?' He pointed his blood-stained blade toward Camelot's surviving knights, many of whom looked ready to keel over. 'Surrender, and I will spare the lives of your gallant men.'

'Never!' Guinevere lofted Sir Ladinas' sword high above the May Day crown nestled atop her raven locks, ready to defend herself.

'As you wish.' Sir Tarquin lunged, swiftly smashing the sword from Guinevere's grasp before reaching out to grab her.

Guinevere swayed left and ran. The giant knight pursued her across the meadow, groping at her with huge, gauntleted hands.

'Away, dog!' Sir Agravain cried. Although bloodied by many wounds, the knight launched himself at his opponent with vigour. A mighty duel ensued. Sir Tarquin, encased in leather, mail and helm, was well protected, and he was powerful. Sir Agravain, too, was strong. Yet, injured as he was, the advantage was Sir Tarquin's. Even so, what Sir Agravain lacked in strength, he gained with unyielding tenacity—and without armour, he was deadly quick.

Sir Agravain attacked Sir Tarquin with all he had. Like a wild animal, the knight of the Round Table hacked and slashed with frightening speed. His sword bashed Sir Tarquin over and over, the blows clattering against his shield or glancing from his armour.

The giant robber knight was unable to combat Sir Agravain's ferocious onslaught and was pushed further and further from the queen.

Sir Agravain struck time and again, stepping after his retreating adversary, allowing him no respite nor a chance to rally.

Suddenly, Sir Tarquin crashed into the grass, his bull-horned helmet torn from his skull. The knight stared into the blue sky, sprawled upon his back. His cheek stung where his opponent's blade had struck, and through dazed eyes, Sir Tarquin watched as the bloodied Sir Agravain strode to finish him. He was at the grim knight's mercy, and by the glint in the man's cold eyes, he was certain there would be none.

Sir Agravain hefted his sword into the air, ready to plunge the blade into the stricken knight's body. Yet before the killing blow fell, Sir Tarquin's horsemen burst between their fallen lord and his foe.

'Finish him!' Sir Tarquin bellowed, his face smeared with blood.

The robber knights levelled their spears at Sir Agravain, who snarled at them like a rabid dog.

'Wait!' Guinevere cried. 'Spare him and those who still live, and I shall go with you of my own free will.' The queen stepped nearer, her demeanour solemn. 'Please, I beg you, Sir Tarquin of Tallyhorn. No more bloodshed. No more death.'

'You cannot, my Queen!' Sir Agravain pleaded desperately.

Guinevere tossed her blade into the meadow, where it lay in the long grass beside the bloodied garlands of her knights and maidens, and with her head bowed, she gave herself to the enemy.

Chapter Three

Sir Galaad le Noir

Again, the great wyrm came for him just as the wretched thing had done a thousand times before. How many deaths had the creature inflicted upon him? He did not know. Too many to count, and each as grisly as the last.

In this twisted twilight existing between life and death, nothing the knight attempted altered his grim fate. The fearsome beast of Corbyn could not be beaten. Yet, this half-life was not always filled with nightmares. He dreamt of his mother and of a blackbird singing at the window. And sometimes, the knight would dream of a maiden so beautiful he found himself not wanting to wake at all. Other times, Guinevere's fair face smiled at him, willing him into the waking world. 'Rise, brave knight. Rise from your rest.'

Arthur haunted the Black Knight the most, even more so than the loathsome wyrm or the army of demons he had fought and slain during his many quests. In his dreams, Arthur's face was forever forlorn. 'Why?' he would ask. 'Why?' And he would ask it over and over. Sometimes, the Black Knight would see Camelot in ruin and the king lying mortally wounded atop his deathbed. 'Look at what you have done,' he would whisper. 'All I have built laid to waste. All I have achieved destroyed. Why?'

The visions plagued the Black Knight's slumber. Day and night merged as one. Time and reality blurred into meaningless. The knight had no concept of where he was nor who cared for him.

The beautiful maiden from his dreams was always present, but so were the terrible wyrm and the red-eyed demons of his past.

The knight's twilight life continued, but in time, the days and nights began to separate, and at last, after what seemed an eternity spent in this other world, he became conscious of his surroundings.

One bright morning, the knight stirred. Linen sheets as white as driven snow covered him. Gingerly, he pushed himself up on weak arms. The bedchamber in which he found himself was as grand as any he had seen. *Truly, this is a magical place*, he thought. *Yet not as enchanting as the fair maiden by my bedside.*

At first, the knight feared he was still sleeping. Flooding through the open window, the warm sun bathed the girl in golden light. Her yellow hair shone like the finest silk, her red lips gleamed like the purest rubies, and her blue eyes sparkled like the brightest stars in the night sky.

'Forgive me,' the Black Knight whispered. 'I thought you a dream, my lady, but here you stand, as real as can be and more beautiful than words can describe.'

The maiden suppressed a titter. 'You flatter me, sir. But mayhap you are yet yourself, and your thoughts do wander foolishly like a leaf upon the wind.'

'It is not flattery; it is the truth. And as for my wellbeing, I feel more alive than ever.'

The maiden eyed the knight dubiously, and once more, the beginnings of a smile flirted with the corners of her mouth.

'You can be none other than Elayne the Fair, daughter of King Pelles, and never has a title been so deserving.'

Ignoring the knight's fawning, Lady Elayne busied herself by refilling her patient's goblet with fresh water. 'What is your name, pray tell?' she asked, pouring the liquid from a crystal pitcher. 'My father only knows you as the fearsome Black Knight, but now that you have risen, perchance you can reveal the truth of the matter?'

The knight accepted the goblet with a grateful nod, and as he took it from her, he brushed her fingers tenderly. 'In truth, my lady, I have forgotten.'

'Forgotten? Or chosen not to remember?' Lady Elayne accused while studying the knight with a scowl. 'The latter, I think. Some past deed haunts you, so you shun who you were to become someone new… someone better.' Abruptly, she realised she had spoken out of turn. 'I am sorry. I know not your plight nor your past and do not wish to intrude or cause offence.' But then she began scowling again. 'Nonetheless, I cannot and will not continue to know you as the fearsome Black Knight, slayer of the diabolical beast of Corbyn. If, indeed, you are a knight?'

'Truly, my lady, you are forgiven on all counts. And knight I am. Also, you are right to think I am haunted by my deeds, but I will embrace my future by honouring my past.'

'Except whatever keeps you from your old life?'

'Except that,' the Black Knight said ruefully.

*

Later, Lady Elayne returned to the Black Knight's bedside with her father, King Pelles, for company. 'A glorious day!' he praised. 'At long last, our saviour has regained his health.'

King Pelles was a tall, broad-shouldered man. His golden hair and beard were wild like a lion's mane but flecked silver with age. Regal robes adorned with a blazing phoenix upon the breast draped his frame, and his eyes shone blue like his daughter's.

'Greetings, King Pelles,' the Black Knight said. He made to rise from his bed, but Lady Elayne was quick to restrain him.

'It is too soon,' she said. 'You must rest.'

The knight slumped into the covers once more. Lady Elayne was right. He did not even have the strength to stand. 'May I ask, for how long have I been in your care?'

King Pelles and his daughter shared an uneasy glance.

'How long?' the Black Knight insisted, but now he feared the answer.

'Summer is spent and the autumn all but over,' King Pelles replied with a sorrowful smile, although he was sure the gesture provided little comfort for his guest. 'I am truly sorry.'

'So long?'

'Alas, it is heavy news to hear,' said King Pelles. 'The old gods and the new have fought for your soul, but it seems you have reason yet to live. Now, you must regain your strength. Please remain for as long as you need. It is the least I can do. In truth, good sir knight, I hoped you might consider staying indefinitely. A man of your bearing would be most welcome at my court.'

The Black Knight's dark gaze fell upon Lady Elayne's sparkling blue eyes, and he was sorely tempted by the king's offer.

'Rest, and if you decide to leave us, you will find your armour restored and enough coin never to want again. You deserve more than I can give. Too many knights and honest folk of Corbyn have I lost to the wyrm. Thanks to your courage, my town, my people, and my daughter are safe. In Merlin's absence, the witch runs amok.'

The witch, Morgana le Fay, had taken offence to King Pelles' claim that his daughter, Lady Elayne, was comelier than any woman alive. In truth, Morgana needed little encouragement to torment her brother's kingdom. Morgana was the High King's half-sister, and she had long lusted for Arthur's crown. She studied the ways of witches and wizards, turning to dark magic to further her cause.

'Thank you, King Pelles. Although, I need no reward. I am sworn to vanquish demons and their masters wherever I find them.'

'You are a knight of the Round Table? A demon hunter?' Lady Elayne asked breathlessly.

The Black Knight nodded. 'Once, yes.'

King Pelles turned to his daughter. 'We are in reputable company indeed, Daughter. A knight of the Round Table! Yet we know not his name.'

'I am Sir Galaad le Noir,' the Black Knight stated.

Lady Elayne raised a questioning eyebrow. 'It appears you have remembered who you are since last we spoke.'

King Pelles stroked his bearded chin in thought. 'I once visited Camelot long ago, and there I met with many of Arthur's great knights.' The king paused, narrowing his blue eyes. 'And although, good sir knight, it is plain to see that you do not wish your true name known, perhaps this old fool stood before you has knowledge of it already?'

Lady Elayne swung to confront her king. 'Who is he, Father?'

King Pelles raised his bushy eyebrows. 'It is not my place to say, Daughter.' Then swiftly did his features become sombre. 'I have further ill tidings to impart, and I urge you, *Sir Galaad le Noir*, to think long and hard before acting in haste.'

The Black Knight's manner hardened. 'Impart your grim tidings, good king. I am ready.'

King Pelles paused. He appeared uncertain whether to reveal his news or not. 'Since the spring, Arthur's queen, Lady Guinevere, has been missing. Some villain has taken her, although there has been no ransom demand.'

The Black Knight's mind unravelled. *What cruel twist of fate is this?* 'But what of Arthur and his knights?'

King Pelles spread his hands. 'I know not. The king has waged war all summer long against the Saxon invaders in the east. I hear that some of Arthur's knights—those who could be spared from the fighting—searched for the queen's whereabouts, but all returned none the wiser.'

At once, the Black Knight rolled from his sickbed, crashing to his knees upon the floor. Nonetheless, with grim determination, he rose and presented himself before his hosts on weak, trembling legs.

King Pelles nodded. 'Elayne, have my steward fetch our guest's armour.'

'Gods have mercy.' Lady Elayne was shocked by her father's request. 'Sir Galaad can barely stand!'

'Do as I say, Daughter.'

'Yes, Father,' Lady Elayne answered meekly. She cast the Black Knight a troubled glance before hurrying from the chamber.

King Pelles appeared downcast. 'Alas, you would have made my daughter and her father happy.' He smiled regretfully. 'But as I feared, your heart belongs to another. And now, Sir Lancelot, the once great champion of Camelot, for the good of the land, you must find her.'

Sir Lancelot was lost for words. For five years or more, he had travelled the length and breadth of Albion, and not once had his true identity been guessed.

King Pelles smiled again. 'Your hair is long, your beard is thick, but these old eyes see all. The way in which a man holds himself says much of who he is. But tell me, why choose Sir Galaad as your new name?'

'If truth be told, it is an old name restored. I was not always Sir Lancelot.' The knight gripped King Pelles' hand. 'I thank you for your understanding, good king,' he said. 'Your daughter is truly the most beautiful maiden in all Albion, but as you say, and to my eternal shame, I love another.'

'Love is above us all, sir knight—kings and queens, lords and ladies, men and maidens. It matters not who you are or where you are from. You cannot hide from it, nor can you run from it. I do not judge you, but others will and not least our king. Yet know this: your secret is safe. Now go, Sir Lancelot! Your armour is ready, and your steed awaits. By the old gods and the new, I wish you good hunting.'

*

Borne upon Cedric, the Black Knight's faithful warhorse, Sir Lancelot rode from King Pelles' castle with a heavy heart. Hunched low in the saddle, he scarcely had strength enough to grip the reins. Yet hope fortified his spirit, and purpose sustained his body.

Sir Lancelot passed through the walled town of Corbyn. Leaving beneath the southern gate, he crossed the thrice-arched bridge spanning the River Evelyn. Pausing halfway, Sir Lancelot traced the river on its sluggish journey beneath the hill on which Corbyn and its castle were built to where it twisted far into the countryside. The river meandered between fair green meadows and autumn woodlands of orange, its banks thick with reeds and rushes and flanked by giant willow trees. Sir Lancelot gazed into the distance. Somewhere out there was Guinevere, and Camelot's lost champion would not rest until he found her.

24

Chapter Four

The Minstrels of Knoberton

For two days and two nights, Sir Lancelot rode south from Corbyn. Late on the third day, as the shadows deepened and the sun fell into the trees of a sprawling forest, he saw an orange glow through the branches.

Cold and weary from his journey, Sir Lancelot urged Cedric toward the distant light. Perchance, there was an opportunity to warm himself by the flames of a fire in the good company of fellow travellers.

Dismounting, Sir Lancelot led his horse into the trees, his right hand lingering over the hilt of his sword. If good company was not to be found, then inevitably, bad would be. The forest was full of robbers, outlaws, and cutthroats—none of which welcomed strangers into their camps.

Winding between the broad trunks of oak and elm, where heel and hoof sank deep into dark, moist soil and warm breath misted in the cool autumn air, Sir Lancelot neared the source of the light. Hearing the muffled sounds of laughter and cheer, the knight's hopes of finding good company and a warm welcome were raised. He found a hollow split by a small woodland stream, and here, Sir Lancelot encountered a party of merry men.

'Oh, no. The gods have mercy,' Sir Lancelot uttered with dread. 'Minstrels.'

Bar none, these merry men appeared ruddy of cheek, round of belly, and jovial of spirit. All were garbed in the brightest colours of the rainbow, and all were as drunk as lords at court. Sir Lancelot was in no mood for minstrels, but it was too late.

'Look here, my good fellows, we have a visitor come to our happy gathering.' The man struggled up from his tree stump perch and swayed precariously, first to his left and then to his right. He carried a horn of ale in one hand and, in the other, a roasted rabbit on a stick. 'Come, friend, join us by the fire. You are most welcome.' Eagerly, he cajoled Sir Lancelot closer. 'Yes, come, come. Eat, drink, rejoice.'

Reluctantly, Sir Lancelot agreed. The smell of roasting rabbit was too good to deny. And besides, drunken minstrels were good for information. In the knight's eyes, it was their only redeeming feature. *These men may have news of interest that might aid my cause.*

Looping the reins of his mount over a tree branch, Sir Lancelot left the animal cropping the tufted grass beneath. The minstrels stood to greet the knight's arrival. Well, they tried to stand, but three of the five failed to accomplish the simple task and instead raised their wineskins in a befuddled salute from where they slumped upon the damp earth.

Sir Lancelot acknowledged the men with a brusque nod before locating himself an upturned log to bear his weight.

'Meat and mead will help put a smile upon your face, good sir knight,' the portliest of the merry men declared. Promptly, a crispy rabbit and a horn of frothy ale were thrust into Sir Lancelot's hands.

'Why so earnest, sir knight? I dare not ask you your name so grim your countenance,' another of the men slurred, and he was by far the drunkest.

Sir Lancelot tipped the horn to his lips and took a long draught of ale. *Not half bad*, he mused in surprise. 'I am earnest and grim, for I am to undertake a perilous quest,' he replied. 'And my name is of little importance.'

'Piffle, sir knight! What is a man without a name? If my good friend will not ask it, then I will, and in return, you shall know mine.'

'Very well,' Sir Lancelot said, too wearisome to debate the issue. 'Some know me as the Black Knight.'

On hearing the stranger's announcement, the minstrels stood—even the three who had tried and failed earlier—and gathered closer to their glum-looking guest.

'Not the Black Knight who slew the Wolf of Arden?' the portliest minstrel asked.

'Not the Black Knight who fought and killed the Creature of Crumbracken?' the most jovial minstrel questioned.

'Not the Black Knight who maimed the Giant Goat of Gorsten Gorge and then married its devilish offspring?' the most inebriated minstrel slurred. The man's merry comrades turned and stared with curious faces. 'Well, so I heard.'

'I am he,' Sir Lancelot answered. 'Although I cannot lay claim to the slaying of this oversized goat you speak of. In truth, the beast sounds more daunting than anything I have yet faced.'

'Your repute is legend, brave sir knight, and believe me when I say it is an honour to find ourselves in your company.' The portly minstrel staggered uncomfortably close, and from his wineskin, he refilled Sir Lancelot's horn. 'My name is Gaston le Grece, and for my many sins, I have found myself the leader of this outfit of motley yet gifted players.' He gesticulated toward what he assumed were his comrades, but in actuality, were the party's horses picketed beside the camp. 'Introducing Pendle, Grenn, Foggy, and Burns. As stout and as good-hearted as any folk in Albion.'

In unison, Gaston's merry men blurted a slurred greeting. Sir Lancelot was left none the wiser to which name belonged to which face.

'Pray tell, Sir Black Knight, what is this dire quest you embark upon that so fills you with woe? Surely a hero such as yourself fears little or nothing at all?' Gaston enquired.

Sir Lancelot smiled wryly before drinking deeply from his horn. 'I only wish that were so. I am charged by King Arthur to find the queen and, gods willing, return her safely to Camelot.'

'The noblest of quests, good sir knight,' the minstrel acknowledged. 'And mayhap, might I venture, your greatest challenge yet?'

'What know you of my quest, minstrel?'

Gaston drained his wineskin and, at once, begged his colleagues for another. 'Only that none have found so much as a hair from the queen's head. Be that as it may, all fingers point to the king's own sister, Morgana le Fay. My advice is to find Morgana, and you find Guinevere. Alas, to face the witch is to face death.'

Indeed, Sir Lancelot thought. Finding Morgana would be no less daunting a task than finding Guinevere. It was well known the witch used dark magic to conceal herself from those who would do her harm.

'On second thought, do not take my advice. Forget the queen—if you are capable of such a deed? Slaying men and monsters is one thing, but confronting a witch as terrible as Morgana le Fay is quite another.' The rosy-cheeked bard shrugged and flung his arms wide, sploshing wine from his replenished skin all over his colleagues. 'I am merely a wandering minstrel who has drunk too much ale and wine. What do I know?'

It appeared the man knew enough to see the dangers of Sir Lancelot's task, and his honesty gave the knight pause for thought. If Guinevere was not so dear to him, would he still accept the quest? *Yes,* he decided. *And while I have not seen Camelot for many a year, I am yet a knight of the Round Table and remain loyal to my king… even if my thoughts for Guinevere betray him daily.*

'Forget your worries, good sir knight,' Gaston said. 'At least for tonight.' Grinning like a mischievous child, the portly minstrel stumbled away to find his steed. The task proved challenging, particularly as it was dark where the horses were stationed and especially as he was having trouble putting one foot in front of the other. Eventually, after much cursing and chortling, he returned to the campfire carrying a lute, which he began plucking playfully.

Realising Gaston's purpose, Pendle, Grenn, Foggy and Burns followed suit and bumbled across the camp to retrieve their own instruments. After a sequence of farcical mishaps involving the fire, a tree trunk, and a horse's hindquarters, the bleary-eyed, red-faced merry men swayed before Sir Lancelot, ready to perform.

The portly Gaston staggered to stand beside the fire. He puffed out his chest like a plump-breasted pigeon, held his lolling head as high as a king, and in a voice loud enough to attract the attention of the forest's robbers, outlaws, and cutthroats, he began.

'Tonight, our fine fellow, the Minstrels of Knoberton present to you,' Gaston performed a stumbling twirl in a valiant attempt to acknowledge his grinning accomplices, 'the most chivalrous, the most heroic, the most gruesome tale of recent times—The Black Knight and the Great Wyrm of Corbyn!'

The morning brought grey skies rolling above the orange leaves of the forest and a sore head and a sour belly for Sir Lancelot.

'Strong ale and cheap wine are not the best bedfellows,' he moaned grimly. Rising gingerly from a bed of moss and twigs, the knight was surprised to find his companions from the previous evening all but ready to break camp and depart.

'At last,' Gaston bellowed. 'The Black Knight rises!' He doused the glowing embers of the fire with a skin of water before saddling his mount. 'We thought you dead, sir knight,' he called over his shoulder, 'but then you began snoring like the Giant Goat of Gorsten Gorge, and we rejoiced at your resurrection!'

'Amen!' the merry men chorused.

'It seems you are destined for greater things and, not least, daring quests of a reckless nature. Yet hear this,' and now the minstrel came to sit beside the knight. 'We journey to the king's tournament at Astolat.'

'Alas,' Pendle added, rocking upon his horse as if he were still submerged up to his eyeballs in ale and wine, 'without the king or his knights!'

'True enough,' Gaston agreed. 'But there will be other knights of renown. And besides, the lords and ladies of Astolat, particularly the ladies, are most generous with their coin and affection. If you have decided to forsake your foolhardy errand, thus preserving your presence here in the land of the living for a time longer, why not accompany us? A knight of your mystery and statue would do well. I dare say your inclusion would pull the crowds—not to mention the maidens. Fame and fortune await you, sir!'

'And us!' Pendle added with a hiccup.

Sir Lancelot shook his head ruefully. 'I do not doubt it, my friends. But, as I think you know, I must face my destiny. Although hiding from it a while longer whilst in the company of such fine fellows is truly tempting. Yet, regretfully, I cannot. Nonetheless, I bid you all a successful and profitable time in Astolat.'

Gaston bowed with a theatrical flourish. 'So be it, sir knight. I wish you well on your noble quest, and let us hope that in the not-too-distant future, the Minstrels of Knoberton shall be recounting the heroic tale of how the Black Knight slew the witch-princess and saved King Arthur's queen.'

*

Overhead, the cloud thickened, and a fine rain drifted from the heavens. Among the autumn forest, enough orange and yellow leaves clung to their branches to ensure Sir Lancelot remained dry. At noon, he stopped to rest. Granting his warhorse the freedom to graze from the abundance of rich foliage blanketing the forest floor, Sir Lancelot leaned his stiff back against the broad trunk of an oak. *I need the rest more than Cedric.* Loosening his waterskin, he drained half the contents in one sitting.

It was simple. To catch a witch, he needed a witch. And none were more fay than Sir Lancelot's own mother, Nimue. She was known as the Lady of the Lake, and she was a powerful witch.

Unlike Morgana, who, deranged with desire and twisted by jealousy, cast her spells to the detriment of others, Nimue used her gifts only to promote the worthy, help the needy, and heal the sick. She was altogether a good witch. Nonetheless, good or evil, folk fear those who are fay, and because of their mistrust, Nimue lived a hermit's life far from the realms of man. But loneliness is a cruel fate even for those blessed with magic.

Tilting his head back, Sir Lancelot finished the last of the water before remounting Cedric. He rode through the hushed forest beneath an ever-darkening sky. The rain came down harder, and the tree branches bent low under the weight of their sodden leaves.

Sir Lancelot pulled the cowl of his black cloak over his dark hair and continued onward, ducking and weaving his way past the drooping, sombre limbs of oak, elm, and birch. The path he trod was overgrown, appearing as nothing more than an animal trail. He smiled fondly. It was his way home.

The hidden route twisted between the trees, winding through the deepest, darkest parts of the forest, the parts folk seldom sought. The terrain was difficult here, and Sir Lancelot was forced from the saddle to lead his stallion through the dense undergrowth.

After a time, the trees thinned, and the trail's tribulations eased, delivering Sir Lancelot to the shoreline of an enclosed woodland lake. Amidst the trees, there was no way of knowing such an expanse of water existed at the forest's heart. Yet here was Sir Lancelot's childhood playground, and beneath the lake's placid surface lived his mother, Nimue.

Chapter Five

The Lady of the Lake

Beside the lake, the forest trees clung to the water's edge, sinking their gnarled roots deep and sending their knotted branches high. On the western shore, beneath an imposing outcrop of moss-covered rock, were dozens of caves. Half-hidden within a thicket of young ash and old oak, the openings peppered the unwelcoming slope like the unblinking black eyes of a giant spider.

On occasion, Sir Lancelot was forced into the cold water to navigate the trees encroaching upon the shore, their long-reaching limbs stretching over the lake. Soon, the caves became more distinct and one among them, the largest, yawned black and ominous like the wide-open maw of a waiting monster.

Fashioned in ancient times, tunnels within the cave ran deep beneath the water—a subterranean habitat hidden from the world above. And for as long as can be remembered, Nimue called this place home.

Before leading his horse from the shore, Sir Lancelot paused, marvelling at the lake's beauty. For a moment, the sun shone between the grey above, and the water's surface shimmered like a sea of glinting emeralds and the surrounding trees, a flaming ring of gold and bronze. Yet the vision was gone as quickly as it appeared, the sun's magnificence banished behind the clouds once more.

Sir Lancelot resumed his journey, climbing through the oak and ash into the gaping black mouth of the biggest cave. The knight's mount whinnied, its wide eyes darting nervously. 'Sssshhh,' Sir Lancelot soothed, patting the animal's neck. 'There is nothing to fear here, Cedric.'

Tying the horse to a stalagmite, Sir Lancelot ventured deeper inside. Hidden amidst the shadowed depths, a rough passage burrowed from sight beneath the ground. The way was lit by a soft, ethereal glow, not magic but nature. A luminous green lichen thrived here beneath the earth, coating the rocks to make the tunnels appear like ghostly gateways to the Otherworld. An effective deterrent to keep curious visitors at bay—nothing put the fear of the gods into folk more than eerie glowing fungi.

Left and right, the passage opened, revealing storerooms, bedchambers, a kitchen stocked with pots, pans, and cauldrons, and a library racked and stacked with parchments and scrolls. Ignoring them, Sir Lancelot continued twisting through the tunnel. He knew precisely where to find his mother. She would be tending her secret garden under the sky.

From the shore, the anomaly was all but invisible to the eye. At the lake's centre was a ring of rock, and within was an opening to the cave system below, breached only by the water where the rock lowered to the north.

Sir Lancelot emerged from the gloomy passage into glorious daylight. Once more, the sun split the clouds asunder, and the Lady of the Lake's subterranean paradise shimmered gold. *It is even more splendid to look upon than I remember*, Sir Lancelot mused, dazzled by the garden's beauty.

Interspersed amidst a lush green lawn stood wild cherry, crab apple, pear, and hazel. Dogwood, spindle, and blackthorn hugged the garden's fringes. A myriad of ever-blooming flowers and shrubs graced the magical environment throughout—bright yellow kingcup, lilac dog rose, blue forget-me-not, fair columbine, and scattered between them, the tiny white and pink petals of enchanter's nightshade. Toadstools sprung from beneath the trees and beside the flowers—jelly ears, shaggy manes, and penny buns. Some edible, some not. Cabbage, parsnip, and leek grew beside pea, bean, and garlic. Potted herbs flourished. Sir Lancelot recognised yarrow, meadowsweet, lovage, and elfwort. There were many more, but he did not know them or had forgotten their names.

Sir Lancelot found his mother sitting beside the pool. As always, the sight of the water cascading from the lake above evoked memories of a childhood spent playing within its enchanted depths.

Nimue dangled her bare feet into the crystal-clear waters. Her silver hair shone like a full moon on a clear night, tumbling the length of her back like the waterfall above. Sir Lancelot opened his mouth to introduce himself, but of course, she already knew he was behind her.

'So, the Black Knight returns,' Nimue said. She withdrew her feet from the pool and faced her son. The witch stood nearly as tall as Sir Lancelot, her serene demeanour expressionless and cold. Nimue's radiant blue eyes narrowed as she studied him.

'Greetings, Mother,' Sir Lancelot said, exhibiting the customary uncertainty he felt when meeting her after a long break. The Lady of the Lake's mood was notoriously challenging to read, even for her son.

'You look peaky,' Nimue announced. 'And rarely have I seen more hair upon a man's face. You could pass as a Northman from beyond the wall.' She pinched his cheek with thumb and forefinger. 'And you have lost weight.'

Sir Lancelot stiffened. 'With good reason,' he declared. 'I have spent the best part of a year banging on Death's door.'

Nimue raised an eyebrow. 'Indeed. I was hoping you would have good cause for neglecting your poor old mother so.'

'Old?' Sir Lancelot replied wryly. 'Mother, you appear no older than I. And as for being poor, there is nothing in this world that you cannot acquire if you wish it—coin or not.'

Nimue's icy exterior thawed and she smiled warmly. 'Welcome home, my son,' she said, drawing Sir Lancelot into an embrace. 'I have missed you so.'

'And I you, Mother,' Sir Lancelot answered, 'but why did you not come?'

Nimue stepped back. 'I did. Do you not remember my song?'

Song? Sir Lancelot vaguely recalled hearing birdsong in the mornings while he lay delirious and half-dead. 'The blackbird.'

'Yes. And if I had not come, the wyrm's poison would have killed you. Elayne the Fair means well, but if left to her own devices, she would have finished you off within a week.'

Sir Lancelot found himself grinning. *Perhaps Lady Elayne would not have made such a good wife after all.*

Nimue beckoned Sir Lancelot to a wooden seat beside the pool. The pew was created from the living branches of hawthorn and honeysuckle bound together.

'So, you have slain another of Morgana's little pets,' Nimue said, settling herself next to her son. 'And a vile little pet at that.'

'Yes. The thing all but killed me. The witch's magic strengthens. How long before she summons a demon that cannot be stopped?'

'Morgana's alliance with the Saxons keeps Arthur's hands tied whilst she runs amok behind his back,' Nimue stated. 'It is she who must be stopped. As her powers increase, the more brazen she becomes.'

'Brazen enough, it seems, to kidnap the queen.'

Nimue cast her sapphire gaze over Sir Lancelot. 'Ah, yes, Guinevere.' She searched her son's dark eyes for a reaction. 'Yet to what end? There have been no terms, no demands, no word at all. Why take the queen and do nothing?'

'I know not. Perchance Morgana hoped to draw Arthur from battle, handing her Saxon friends a greater foothold in the east?' Sir Lancelot suggested.

'Perhaps.' Nimue fell silent and, for a time, stared into the water's depths. 'I fear she plays another game. Morgana is not yet powerful enough to challenge Arthur, not while he commands Excalibur, and she may never be. Nonetheless, if her brother were to be weakened in some way, then mayhap she would be able to even the odds.'

Sir Lancelot grasped Nimue's hands. 'Where is the witch hiding, Mother? Show me.'

Nimue shook her head. 'I cannot say. A darkness has descended over the land, a veil of evil I cannot penetrate. And if I did know, I am not certain I would tell you.'

Sir Lancelot was taken aback by his mother's words. 'Why would you not? I do not understand?'

Nimue studied her son once more. 'Tread carefully,' she whispered. 'You have much to gain but more to lose. Your role in Arthur's future, in Albion's future, is written in the stars. Yours and Arthur's destinies are entwined, but you must be his saviour, not his doom. Albion's fate teeters on the brink, and come the end, I know not which way she shall fall.'

Abruptly, Sir Lancelot stood. 'I care not for prophecies,' he blustered, startling a murder of crows into flight from the treetops. 'If you will not help me, I know another witch who might.'

'Hellawes?' Nimue hissed. 'Do not be a fool. She would sooner see you dead than help you. The Saxon witch cannot be trusted. Her use of dark magic is abhorrent, an abomination against the living.' The Lady of the Lake paused to think. 'Yet, one so corrupt and steeped in evil may be able to unveil Morgana's shroud.' Nimue sighed heavily. 'Fate cannot be cheated,' she whispered sadly. 'Hellawes will want something in exchange for such knowledge, and I fear the price will be high.'

'I am prepared to pay,' Sir Lancelot answered.

'We shall see.' Nimue slipped a silver ring from a finger and presented it to her son. 'Take this,' she said. 'It will help shield you against dark magic.'

Sir Lancelot accepted the gift gratefully. 'Thank you, but the ring is too small.'

Nimue smiled, and the witch's blue eyes blazed. 'Then wear it close to your heart.' A fresh shoot of honeysuckle uncoiled from the pew. The plant gathered the ring from the knight's palm, threading the silver artefact to its length before looping itself around Sir Lancelot's neck. Having accomplished its task, the honeysuckle shoot snapped free, withdrawing once more to the seat.

'The cord will not be easily broken,' Nimue declared. 'Keep the ring near for its power to protect you.' She took Sir Lancelot's hands in hers. 'There is much at stake and much you do not yet know. I sense an evil approaching that, if unchecked, threatens to engulf all within its path. Be watchful, but do all you can to stem the tide. Morgana le Fay is the key.'

'Will the druids not answer your call?' Sir Lancelot queried, troubled by his mother's grim foretelling. He could not recall seeing her so fearful.

'The druids are not the force they once were. The Romans saw to that. They linger still in the west, hiding among the mountains and forests.' Nimue smiled wistfully. 'If Merlin can be found, perhaps they will rise again, but I fear Merlin's time on this earth is spent, and he has returned to whence he came.'

Sir Lancelot appeared grave but steadfast. 'Then it is up to those of us who remain to make a stand.'

'Yes,' Nimue said proudly. 'You have my ring to aid you; now give me your sword.'

Sir Lancelot unsheathed his blade and, hilt first, offered the weapon to the Lady of the Lake. Taking the sword, Nimue carried it directly into the crystal pool, where she held the blade under the rushing waterfall.

'Excalibur is the sword of kings, the sword of the Chosen, forged by gods not of this world, and it knows no equal. Yet there are other weapons of power and other means by which to forge them.'

Again, the witch's eyes pulsed a piercing blue, and for a time, so did the pool and water cascading from above. At last, Nimue pulled the sword from the waterfall, and its blade shone silver like the hair atop the witch's head. 'Behold,' she proclaimed, 'Secace—Sword of Shining!'

Chapter Six

The Bargain

Sir Lancelot travelled east in search of the Saxon witch, Hellawes. Winter's grip tightened, the days grey and the nights cold. Atop Cedric, the Black Knight rode through the heart of Albion. Enduring wind, rain, and snow, he wandered golden forests and emerald pastures, trekked over grassy hills and rugged highlands, and crossed rampant rivers and sprawling meadows, wild and untamed.

Sir Lancelot sheltered from howling gales and thundering storms beneath barren branches or inside the dark mouths of upland caves. He spent his nights huddled beside his horse, wrapped within the depths of his cloak upon beds of fallen leaves.

The journey was long and arduous, but Sir Lancelot felt his strength returning with each day's dawn. At last, it seemed, he was free of the wyrm's poison.

For a time, the knight trod the Roman road eastward, straight and true. Yet the route was busy with the comings and goings of Arthur's war against the Saxons. He encountered soldiers, knights and their squires, and sometimes monks and messengers, but more often than not, supply wagons ferrying goods to the high king's army.

Before leaving the road, Sir Lancelot spoke with a wagon master returning from the war, 'What news?'

'The fighting is fierce, and the battle rages like a never-ending winter storm. The enemy's ranks are filled with giants and trolls, and their warriors fight with savage hunger.'

'How does the king fair?'

'Well enough. The king smites all who challenge him… man or monster—Excalibur fells them all. Yet, the enemy is relentless and fearless. Day after day, they come. I fear Arthur and his army will soon grow weary and falter.'

A day later, Sir Lancelot saw for himself from the summit of a grassy hillock. Arthur's army was strung across a rising slope above a wide, fast-flowing river below him in the valley. On the opposite bank, the Saxons assembled, preparing themselves for another attack.

Sir Lancelot could see no trolls, but seldom had he witnessed so many fighting men set for battle. Among them towered lumbering giants armed with the trunks of uprooted trees and howling dire wolves as big as horses.

I should be fighting at Arthur's side.

Bloated and fat, carrion crows circled the skies above, waiting for the dead to litter the battlefield and the feast to begin again. Sir Lancelot did not stay to watch. He turned his mount aside and continued eastward with Saxon battle cries ringing in his ears and guilt weighing heavily upon his shoulders.

Twice on the following day, Sir Lancelot was forced from the path by Saxon warbands. On each occasion, a party of mounted men—twenty strong and equipped with mail and spear—rode their steeds perilously close to Sir Lancelot's hiding place, the first of which was among a tight grove of rowan trees and the second beneath a vast humped barrow of the dead.

The rolling hills gave way to a flat, broad, and featureless land—a place of bleak, lonely horizons and insect-infested bogs. A chilling mist rose with every dawn, the sky above as grey as stone, the terrain a grim and hopeless landscape to endure. Sir Lancelot rode for miles and miles, his surroundings seeming never to alter. It was almost as if he moved not at all. *Have faith. Hellawes is near.* Nimue's enchanted ring compelled him toward the witch's abode, drawn to her dark magic.

The next morning, driven by a desire to be rid of this cursed land, Sir Lancelot broke camp early. Above, the weather was as joyless as ever. The oppressive sky promised sleet or snow, and the grey mists, so prevalent a feature here in this soulless landscape, rolled thick and icy-cold across the flatlands.

The sun climbed behind the churning clouds, and Sir Lancelot trudged ever onward. A squally shower passed over, and another soon after. As a third downpour eased, a distant haze caught Sir Lancelot's eye. Not cloud or mist but a rising smog. Drawing near, the knight saw that it was cast from a dreary timber hall, slumped black and forlorn on the leaden skyline.

Plodding between pools of stinking, fly-plagued swamps and swaths of sodden, stagnant earth, Sir Lancelot approached the ruinous hall with trepidation. The drab structure would have blighted its surroundings in any other part of Albion, but not here. Here, it was well-suited to its bleak environment.

Hellawes' hall was a rotting carcass of timber beams. Perchance, it was once a residence of repute belonging to a man of wealth but now home to a madwoman with a grim fascination for the dead. There were no guards at the door, and if not for the billowing smoke lifting through the decomposed thatch and flame-blackened rafters, there would have been no sign of life within at all.

Knotting Cedric's reins to the withered branch of a stunted ash tree, Sir Lancelot slowly pushed open the door. A loud, high-pitched squealing pierced the grim, lonely silence. Sir Lancelot cursed.

A wild cackling greeted the Black Knight's entrance. Hellawes huddled beside the hearth astride a knotted throne of oak, its rotted legs submerged in puddles of murky rainwater. 'At last, my sweet Sir Lancelot has returned to me. If I recall, when last we met, you left me for dead?'

'A long time ago, Princess.'

The hall's interior was as woeful as its exterior—dismal and gloomy, ripe with the smell of death. It was larger than it appeared from the outside. Although so barren of furnishings and adornments, the dreary place felt more extensive than it was. Beams of pale light lanced through the many gaps in the roof and walls, highlighting a collection of animal bones strewn across the floor. *The witch is no better than the wrym,* he thought, reminded of the creature's terrible lair.

Gingerly, Sir Lancelot stepped toward the fire where Hellawes warmed herself by the flames, petting a raven perched upon her bony knees like a faithful hound. She appeared no better than the building she called home. The witch's flaxen hair was wild and filth-ridden, her face gaunt and limbs thin. *She is all skin and bone.* Hellawes looked as if she rarely ate, and when she did, Sir Lancelot guessed her meals consisted of nothing but birds, rats and spiders.

For all her repulsive attributes, which were many, underneath the grime and filth caking her scrawny body from head to toe,

Princess Hellawes was a rare beauty. She was the daughter of Arthur's enemy, the Saxon king, Hengist—or was it Horsa? Sir Lancelot seldom remembered. Either way, she was another cursed witch princess, the same as Morgana le Fay.

'I like what you have done with the place,' Sir Lancelot mocked, casting his eyes over the hall's dilapidated state. 'Airy with a natural feel.'

Hellawes sniggered. 'Most observant, my love. What is more natural than death and decay?'

Sir Lancelot's fingers sought the hilt of his sword. 'There is nothing natural about what you do here, Hellawes.'

'What is so wrong with trying to unlock the eternal secrets of life and death?'

'Some secrets are not for knowing.'

The witch hissed like a snake. 'I despise Arthur and his righteous knights. Your new god makes me sick. You preach compassion and forgiveness but slaughter all who oppose you, demanding the obedience of all the gods. But I tell you this, Woden will never bow!' The maddened witch spat into the fire, her foul phlegm sizzling in the flames.

Hellawes' blue eyes narrowed. 'Why have you come, Lancelot? Wait. Let me guess,' she said, cackling again. 'You have come to ask for my help. You want me to find your precious Guinevere for you, do you not?' Abruptly, the witch's mirth stopped, and she stared at Sir Lancelot with fierce longing burning in her eyes. 'Why would I help you? If Guinevere dies, mayhap you will love me in her stead.'

'I will love Guinevere no less in death than in life, witch.'

Hellawes sneered. 'How sweet.' Shoving the raven to the rotted rushes, she rose from her throne. 'Do you know why I choose to live here?'

'I can only assume you enjoy the solitude.'

'You think I am alone?' Hellawes whispered, her expression haunted, her eyes distant. 'I am never alone. The ghosts of the dead keep me company.' She pointed a long, black fingernail toward the open door that groaned back and forth on the breeze. 'This place is an ancient burial ground. That is why I choose to live here—an endless source of old bones and willing corpses to satisfy my needs. Yet there are other things buried deep down, claimed by the bogs and marshes. Things long dead. Things that no longer walk this earth. Would you like to meet such a thing?'

Sir Lancelot edged away from Hellawes, her eyes gleaming feverishly. 'So, you will not help me?'

The witch tilted her head sideways, her knotted locks falling across her face like matted straw. Hellawes pressed a bony finger to her black-stained lips as if pondering a decision she had yet to make, even though she already had. 'I think not,' she said. 'In truth, Lancelot, *I am* alone. And that is why I have decided you shall stay and become my soulmate.'

Sir Lancelot spun and made all haste for daylight. Yet the hall's creaking door slammed shut before the knight's arrival, denying his escape.

'Please stay,' Hellawes implored. 'We shall make such a lovely couple, you and I.' Exhibiting a downturned mouth with wide, baleful eyes to match, the witch mimicked a sad face. Then her lips kinked into a sinister sneer.

Sir Lancelot drew Secace, thrusting the shining sword before him with both hands. The enchanted weapon's silver blade shrouded the knight in a haze of shimmering light.

Screaming, Hellawes cowered from the luminous glare but swiftly cast her spells upon the earth beneath her feet. Tendrils of twisting black smoke tore from the witch's scrawny frame, swirling like wraiths among the rotted beams above her head. Then, one after the other, the plumes of shadow plummeted, vanishing deep beneath the cursed ground.

'Halt whatever it is that you do,' Sir Lancelot implored. 'I am prepared to strike a bargain!'

Hellawes cackled wilder than ever, exulting in her power. The earth shook, and the old hall trembled. 'Why should I bargain when I can take whatever I desire?'

From the soil below burst great jutting bones that launched into the air. Suspended between the rushes and the rafters, the relics floated toward Hellawes.

Sir Lancelot watched the scene unfold with terrible curiosity as a vast skeletal body began taking shape. A monstrous ribcage formed around the witch, cocooning her within. More and more bones erupted from the ground to complete the unholy puzzle. An enormous, elongated jaw lined with dagger-like teeth protruded from a gigantic skull, and behind its once-powerful legs, a spiked tail swung from side to side. Where the creature's eyes once shone, orbs of red now burned bright amongst the gloom of Hellawes' hall. The long-dead monster's skeletal wingtips stretched so wide they tore through the decaying walls. And even though the beast was nothing more than thin air and bone, its roar was as real as the day it died.

'A dragon,' Sir Lancelot gasped. 'A dragon of bones!'

From within the beast's skeletal frame, Hellawes commanded her resurrected servant to do her bidding. The dragon's fearsome head lunged at the horrified knight, but Nimue's ring flared blue, enveloping her son within a pulsing light. The dragon's colossal jaw crunched against the knight's enchanted shield, and all at once, its ancient teeth shattered into dust.

Hellawes' screams issued from the ramshackle hall, echoing loud and clear across the bleak landscape beyond. Mad with rage, the witch released her spell, returning the dragon's tormented soul to the Otherworld and sending its earthly bones crashing to the rushes.

The radiant blue light emanating from Nimue's ring faded. Sir Lancelot sheathed his silver sword, sensing the danger was past.

'Now we bargain,' Hellawes announced nonchalantly. She returned to her throne, seating herself beside the fire once more. 'My price is this: I will help, and as a result of my help, you shall have Guinevere's love in life, and I shall have yours in death. To seal the deal, I require a kiss from my betrothed.'

'Agreed.' Sir Lancelot did not flinch, but inside, he felt as if Hellawes had ripped out his still-beating heart. *What am I doing?* he thought despairingly. *What must be done.*

Striding to Hellawes, the knight bent low to find her cracked lips.

The witch ran her bony fingers through the knight's dark, tangled hair. Digging her nails into his scalp, she pulled his mouth against hers and kissed Sir Lancelot with passion. Her blackened tongue slithered between his lips, squirming inside his mouth like a wriggling eel caught in a net.

Gagging, Sir Lancelot pushed himself away.

'I look forward to your death, my love,' Hellawes whispered seductively, licking Sir Lancelot's blood from her red lips.

Sir Lancelot spat before wiping his mouth with the back of his hand. 'Now tell me where I can find Guinevere,' he demanded. 'The bargain is made.'

'Of course, my love.'

Hellawes snatched the raven from the rotted boards and, in a frenzied attack, tore open the unsuspecting bird with claw-like nails until its innards lay strewn across her lap. Hunched double, the witch studied the raven's bloodied remains, jabbing and poking at the organs and offal with her stained fingers.

'Well?' Sir Lancelot prompted, trying his utmost not to let his disgust tell.

Hellawes grunted with dissatisfaction. Then, jerking her head up, she met the knight's gaze. 'Guinevere resides in the west. I know not where.' She stared back at the guts before probing them with a finger once more. 'A tower in the wild woods.'

Suddenly, Hellawes shook and trembled, clawing at her head. 'Morgana's magic clouds my thoughts!'

'You waste my time.' Sir Lancelot turned to leave. 'The deal is off.'

'Wait! There is more. Find the brute who bears the scar. You will know him when the time comes. Pursue this knight to his master, and you shall discover your precious queen. Be warned, Nimue's ring is no match against Morgana le Fay. I despise her but would not cross her, not even with an army of undead dragons at my side.'

'Your concern is touching. Where do I find this brute?'

'Not concern, merely advice. I would hate for you to be denied Guinevere's love, knowing that without it, I must forsake my own after your death. Search for him at Astolat.'

'Astolat? There is a tournament there this winter solstice.'

'Yes. Call it fate or destiny or whatever you want, but this man seeks you out. It should make life easier for you.'

Sir Lancelot nodded. 'Until we meet again, witch-princess.'

'I look forward to it more than you can know,' Hellawes rasped.

49

Chapter Seven

Demands

'More than half a year has passed, and still, he has not come for her,' Lord Mellegrans stated.

'He will come,' Morgana reassured. 'Patience, my lord.'

Lord Mellegrans rested a gloved hand on the rough, grey stone of the parapets, and with a dejected stare, he gazed out across the sprawling forest. The trees disappeared into the distance like an endless army of twisted giants. Lord Mellegrans could not decide whether the forest was guarding the tower or preparing to lay siege to it. 'We were naïve to assume Arthur would place his queen above his people. He is married to duty before he is married to his wife. Are you certain the ransom demand was made?'

Morgana felt compelled to shove the pathetic, lecherous man over the edge. Short, balding, and incapable of independent thought, Lord Mellegrans was a snivelling lecherous swine. *But a swine with wealth*, she reminded herself.

'I am certain, my lord. I saw the demands despatched myself,' she lied. There was no ransom demand, nor would there ever be.

Morgana knew full well that her brother would not come. Yet that was never her intention. She only deceived Lord Mellegrans into thinking it was. He would not understand the subtleties required to maximise their good fortune. When Arthur marched his army against the Saxons, Morgana had been keen to strike while the king's back was turned.

Guinevere had always been a target, but she was forever guarded and seldom did she abandon the safety of Camelot. Yet when word reached Morgana's ever-listening ears of the queen's intentions to leave Albion's stronghold in favour of a day spent frolicking in the countryside, Morgana's interest was pricked.

Grudgingly, Morgana gave Lord Mellegrans and his knights their due. They had executed the abduction faultlessly, all be it suffering heavy losses. Not that Morgana cared. Soldiers were easy to come by; their lives meant nothing to her.

'Should I increase the guards manning the gates?' Lord Mellegrans questioned nervously. 'And are you sure we should not build fortifications? Mayhap a sentry tower or a perimeter wall? Perchance a ditch?'

Mellegrans was concerned. The tower appeared woefully unprotected.

'No,' she replied. *Fool. It matters not how many soldiers guard the gates nor how high the walls stand.* No one would find them here. Her magic cloaked their presence—at least, for now.

I need more time. The spell Morgana crafted was crucial to her plans but complex and troublesome to cast. Commanding the elements and summoning demons from the Otherworld was one thing, but altering human form was quite another. Yet, she was so very near.

Manipulating men in positions of power was child's play for Morgana. Feed them false promises and show them a heaving bosom, and they were putty in her hands. *And if all else fails*, she thought with a wry smile, *bewitch them.*

'Yes, of course, my lady,' Lord Mellegrans stammered, feeling foolish for suggesting such a thing. 'But what if Arthur sends an army?'

Morgana despaired. 'We have talked about this, my lord. Arthur's army is fighting the Saxons, and the kings who remain behind care nothing for Guinevere, only for the contents of their coffers and the security of their borders. Nonetheless, if it eases your fears, by all means, strengthen the garrison. Arthur will come, and if he does not, he will send another in his place. Either way, we win.'

Morgana smiled with satisfaction. She could not beat Arthur in battle, not yet, but there were other ways to dethrone a king and win a war.

Flakes of snow began dancing from the steel grey skies. Morgana watched Lord Mellegrans pull his thick fur cloak around his corpulent frame. 'Let us go inside,' he suggested. 'The cold must be dreadfully uncomfortable for you to bear, my lady.' The man's hungry eyes scanned Morgana's shapely form, paying particular attention to areas of exposed flesh.

Morgana's green eyes blazed with contempt. Yes, she dressed provocatively to hold his interest, but it did not stop her from cringing at the thought of what was going on inside his sordid mind. Tall, curvy, and blessed with cascading black curls, sparkling emerald eyes and soft silken skin, she knew she was beautiful, and the dark magic coursing through her body only enhanced that beauty further.

In truth, Morgana had no need for capes and furs. She could happily parade naked in the eye of an ice storm without developing so much as a goosebump. It was one of many advantages enjoyed as a servant of the Infernal Shadow.

'Yes, let us retreat inside,' Morgana answered. For good measure, she feigned a shiver and wrapped her arms beneath her chest, rubbing at her bare skin with her hands. 'The winter air freezes my heart.' *When I am queen, I will have no need of men such as Mellegrans.* Inwardly, she grinned. *I will enjoy watching his fat, hog-like body roasting over the eternal fires of Hell.* Yet, for now, she needed him.

Escaping the snowstorm, the pair ducked into a narrow, winding staircase.

'Will you be staying the night, my lady?' Lord Mellegrans asked eagerly.

Despite her indomitable self-control, Morgana could do nothing to suppress a shudder. The unwelcome sensation was not born of the cold but from the repulsive thought of spending the foreseeable future in the man's repugnant presence. Yet, having discovered the spell's final secret, she would not be going anywhere. 'Yes, my lord. With your consent, I shall remain here until our business is concluded.'

*

Too few to be a Warband, Sir Lancelot mused, gazing into the murky distance. He counted six men. *A scouting party?*

Unlike Sir Lancelot's previous encounters with Saxon patrols, the open country here offered nowhere to hide. He considered making a dash for it, but with Cedric burdened with supplies and a long journey ahead, sooner or later, they would catch him. *Better to choose my ground and make a stand,* he thought. Not that one piece of ground looked any different to another in this drab place, which was precisely the reason why the terrain was so treacherous to traverse.

Sir Lancelot chose a suitably hazardous area and prepared for his meeting with the Saxons. He loosened the straps securing his shield and helmet to Cedric. Then, after removing the heavy cloak from around his broad shoulders, he pulled on his mail gauntlets and waited.

An icy wind cut through the flatlands from the east. Sir Lancelot shivered. For an instant, he considered refastening his cloak but decided feeling cold was preferable to being dead. *The garment hampers my movement and speed in battle.* And besides, there was nothing like a bracing gale to heighten the senses and focus the mind.

Sir Lancelot watched the Saxons plot a route through the landscape. Sometimes, the bogs were deceptive and difficult to detect until it was too late. Escaping their foul clutches was a tiresome and, on occasion, forlorn task. Criss-crossing towards him, the warriors disturbed bitterns and marsh warblers into the air, the small birds tweeting furiously as they struggled against the gusting winds.

The thumping of hooves carried to Sir Lancelot's ears, and soon enough, he saw the animals' hot breath misting in the cold air. The leader of the scouting party—Sir Lancelot ascertained this because he alone among them wore a helmet—rode at the centre of the Saxons, a green cape billowing behind him. Each of the six men held a long spear in one hand and their reins in the other.

Good, no archers, Sir Lancelot thought. A well-crafted bow in the hands of a skilled veteran could be a deadly asset, especially in open terrain with little to no cover.

The Saxons halted short of Sir Lancelot, who had placed himself on the opposite side of a bog thick with reeds and rushes. 'What business have you in our lands, knight?' the leader of the patrol queried. The Saxon was a big man with a big beard. In addition to a fine helmet, he wore an expensive coat of mail, and Sir Lancelot spotted a longsword at his side.

'I sought the company of Princess Hellawes,' Sir Lancelot answered. 'And my business with her is none of your concern.'

To a man, the Saxons gawped at Sir Lancelot as if he had just slain a dragon—which, of course, he had… at least a dead one.

'The witch? You are brave indeed to have faced and survived a meeting with that demented hag. Why did she let you live?'

Sir Lancelot shrugged his shoulders. 'I gave her a kiss.'

The Saxons chuckled amiably. 'I like you, knight,' the leader said. 'Yet even though you speak our tongue well enough, clearly you are a Briton. And as a Briton caught on Saxon soil, we require you to pay a tax.' The Saxon's greedy gaze fell to the sword secured at Sir Lancelot's hip. 'As you made us laugh, your blade will suffice.' But then he glimpsed the silver ring on its honeysuckle cord, hung about the knight's neck. 'And the little trinket that you keep hidden beneath your mail.'

Sir Lancelot smiled. 'I think not,' he said. 'You will have neither the sword nor the ring and nothing in their stead. Ride on, and your lives will be spared.'

The Saxons roared with laughter, and while they did so, Sir Lancelot slid his helm over his head, strapped his black shield to his left forearm, and drew Secace.

On seeing the knight's silver sword, the leader and his men cut short their mirth. 'You jest, Briton? Six against one are not favourable odds, even if you do wield a pretty blade.'

The Saxons began sniggering again.

'True enough,' Sir Lancelot agreed. 'You ought to have brought more men.'

The leader's face turned cruel. 'You three, go that way!' he hissed, kicking his horse into action. 'You two, with me!'

Not risking the bog, the Saxons split their numbers to come at the knight from two sides at once. Yet, Sir Lancelot had chosen his ground wisely, and the big leader and his men floundered in no man's land, their horses knee-deep in marsh water.

Squeezing his thighs, Sir Lancelot wheeled Cedric to face the other Saxon attack. The three warriors lacked the space to charge at him full tilt, and without the impact created by such momentum, Sir Lancelot was able to fend their spears away with sword and shield. The Saxon warriors circled, thrusting their weapons at him from their saddles.

A spear glanced from Sir Lancelot's armour, and then another clattered against the iron boss of his shield. As the third Saxon spear jabbed toward him, he struck.

Flashing bright, Secace slashed the weapon in two. Then, sweeping thrusting spears aside, Sir Lancelot cut the Saxons from their saddles one after the other.

Witnessing the swift demise of their comrades, the remaining Saxon warriors wheeled their steeds about and, in all haste, galloped from the scene.

Sir Lancelot sighed. He knew he ought to pursue them, lest they return with a warband, but he had seen enough death and despair for one day. He sheathed Secace. *I will take my chances.* Stowing his helmet and shield, he draped his black cloak around his shoulders, and as the crows gathered overhead, he rode west.

The wind howled, and the sky above grew dark. Snow was coming, and it was many days to Astolat.

Chapter Eight

Astolat

The day was late, and the skies black. Wet sleet swept eastward on raw winds.

With his cowl drawn tight and head bent low, Sir Lancelot rode his steed through Astolat's dark, abandoned streets. In daylight and in less foul weather, Astolat was a bustling market town like Corbyn. Arthur's peace had brought prosperity. Trade flourished, inns thrived, and for most, life was bearable. No longer did the ravagers come; no more did the people grow cold and hungry.

Sir Lancelot's eyes were drawn to the castle. It towered above the town like a monstrous stone guardian watching over all who sheltered beneath. It shone like a beacon in the storm, its white walls illuminated by hundreds of flickering lights.

'A lamentable sight,' Sir Lancelot mused wistfully.

The gusting wind tugged at him like a pack of hungry wolves intent on pulling him from the saddle. Wrapping his cloak tight, he sighed. In times past, Camelot's champion occupied pride of place at Lord Astolat's table. Sir Lancelot lowered his gaze from the castle, just as he had learnt to lower his expectations in life. *No more am I the honoured guest*, he told himself. *Now, I am but a hunter of demons.*

Although no longer privy to the society's meetings, Sir Lancelot's vow to the Order of the Round Table held true. In fact, during his self-imposed exile, he had hunted and slain more demons than ever before. Consumed by glorious purpose, he had become hell-bent, focusing his energies on honouring his pledge. Deep inside, he questioned whether his dedication to the cause was payment for his sins. *How many good deeds will my conscience require before it is appeased? How many demons must I vanquish before I am forgiven?*

The sleet eased, yet the bracing east wind persisted. Sir Lancelot stopped beside a busy inn. At a glance, the place appeared as good as any other. He eyed the sign swinging in the breeze above the weathered door: The Blushing Maiden. A picture of a flush-faced wench greeted him, beckoning him inside with a sly smile, a heaving bosom, and a mischievous wink. Alas, an area of paint had long since flaked away, leaving the poor girl with but one good eye and half a nose. *Fortuitously, her bosom remains intact,* Sir Lancelot mused, allowing himself a wry smile.

Suddenly, the door beneath the half-blind wench burst open. A raucous din accompanied a stumbling, bleary-eyed man whose pallor was best described as the opposite of healthy. Promptly, the man disgorged the contents of his stomach onto the wet ground, and he did so with such violence that Cedric's forelegs fell prey to the drunk's vomitus splatter.

Grim-faced, Sir Lancelot kicked his mount onward. 'Come, Cedric. The Blushing Maiden is not for us.'

The knight passed two subsequent inns without pause. It appeared the tournament had attracted many to the town, all seemingly intent on filling their bellies with beer and their ears with tasteless music. Finally, a third inn offered hope. A warm, welcoming glow issued from the premises, and there was no hint of a horn or pipe to be heard. Despite its name, Sir Lancelot concluded that the Tipsy Squire was an altogether more civilised establishment than those previously encountered in Astolat.

'This will do,' Sir Lancelot declared, patting Cedric's neck.

Adjacent to the inn was a stable yard. A tall, reedy youth materialised from the dismal night carrying a lantern that spluttered and spat in the wind. Sir Lancelot dismounted, and after gathering his possessions—namely his helmet, shield, and provisions—he handed Cedric's reins to the stable hand.

'Be careful, boy. He bites,' Sir Lancelot warned gruffly.

The boy looked petrified of both horse and knight.

'I jest,' Sir Lancelot said, forcing his face into a grin. He tossed the boy a coin. 'For your trouble.'

Sometimes, he forgot how intimidating his appearance had become. Having lived a solitary life for so long, he had grown accustomed to his wild aspect. After all, according to his mother, there were Northmen beyond the wall groomed better than he. As for Cedric, well, he was a warhorse, and as such, it was his job to look intimidating.

Far from being convinced by the knight's reassurances, the stable hand—at arm's length and as fast as he could manage—steered the black charger warily into the shelter.

Sir Lancelot crossed the windswept yard and, hoping to avoid unnecessary attention, gained access to the Tipsy Squire via a small rear entrance. Inside, the knight found himself within an ill-lit and ill-designed passage that was neither wide enough nor high enough to navigate without turning sideways while bent double like a hunchback. The helmet cradled beneath his left arm scraped the walls, and the shield slung across his back bashed against the beams.

The knight's discomfort soon ended, and the passage deposited him into a spacious, welcoming hallway. Ahead, a staircase wound upwards to bedrooms above, and beyond the hall, Sir Lancelot spotted a common room. From within, soft, amiable chatter, occasionally punctuated by friendly laughter, was accompanied by the smell of pipe smoke and roasted meats.

Sir Lancelot promised himself a tankard of ale and a platter of whatever wafted so invitingly in the air before the night was over.

A well-worn counter, accessed by a hinged side hatch, occupied the space beneath the twisting staircase. Attached to the wall behind the desk was an arrangement of shelves, hooks, and cubbyholes where parchments, keys, and customers' valuables were stored for the duration of their stay.

Sir Lancelot raised his eyebrows. He doubted the Tipsy Squire's patrons trusted the innkeeper with their possessions—not if they had any sense. The counter was the only thing preventing a thief from ransacking the wooden boxes and claiming whatever was hidden inside. Sir Lancelot shook his head. The hinged side hatch had been left open. The proprietor was either incompetent or a gullible fool.

Sir Lancelot berated himself. *I have spent far too long in my own company.* Now, it seemed he only found the faults in men and not their strengths.

Dropping his saddlebags, Sir Lancelot placed his helmet on the counter before ringing the miniature brass bell provided. For such a small device, the bell rang loud and true.

At once, the common room quietened. 'Farley,' Sir Lancelot heard a man say, 'you're needed out front. Sounds like you've got yourself a screamer.' Moments later, with the chatter in the common room restored, a tall, thin man ducked through the doorway and into the hall.

'My apologies,' said the man, hurrying behind the counter. He produced a dirty rag from a shirt sleeve and duly dabbed perspiration from his endless forehead. 'I am short-staffed tonight. The chef's assistant has gone down with the pox, or something like it and just as nasty, so muggins here has become chief bottle washer and cook.' He shook his balding head. 'And this of all weeks. The tournament is our busiest time of year!' Farley took a breath and eyed the scruffy, bearded man on the other side of the counter. Farley frowned. 'Are you taking part on the morrow?'

'Perhaps,' Sir Lancelot replied. 'I have yet to decide.'

Farley nodded as if the knight's answer confirmed his suspicions. 'Freelancer, hey? Well, you'll have no shortage of lords and ladies to tout your services to. I doubt if there's a single noble in Albion who isn't here. Save for good King Arthur, of course. Praise his name! Fighting on our behalf while we make merry. It doesn't feel right, does it?'

Not for the first time since Sir Lancelot's exile, he felt unbearable guilt crushing his soul. 'I require a room for the week and stabling for my mount.' He had little patience for the man's idle chit-chat. *I need that drink.* 'Are your stables secure?' he asked, glancing once more at the poorly protected deposit boxes behind the innkeeper. 'My horse is dear to me.'

Farley took offence. He stretched himself to his full height—well, at least until his hairless crown bumped against a particularly knobbly beam—and narrowed his eyes with indignation. 'I can assure you, sir knight, that I run a tight ship here at the Squire. Nothing gets past my boy, Barley.'

Like father like son, Sir Lancelot mused. Both were tall, stooping men as thin as rakes. Although Farley had grown a perfectly round potbelly that would have unquestionably been mistaken for evidence of imminent motherhood if he were of the fairer sex.

'I did not mean to cause offence,' Sir Lancelot apologised. He placed a handful of coins on the counter. 'If you have a room, I would be most grateful.' In truth, Cedric was capable of fending for himself. A trained warhorse was not so easily stolen.

'Of course,' Farley answered, and as the man relaxed, his stoop returned. The innkeeper offered his hand for shaking. 'Farley Butterman at your service.'

'Sir Galaad le Noir, at yours,' Sir Lancelot replied, grasping the man's sweaty palm.

'Sir Galaad le Noir? The Black Knight! Good gracious me, sir! Why did you not say sooner? You honour me with your custom. You shall have my finest room!'

'That will not be necessary,' Sir Lancelot assured, cringing. *How is my name so well known when I wander the realm alone?*

Ignoring Sir Lancelot's words and coin, Farley Butterman began fussing with the keys hanging on their hooks. 'Here we are, room nine,' he announced, claiming a large iron key. 'The best room in the house!'

Sir Lancelot took the key with a grateful nod before gathering his things.

'If there is anything I can do for you, just ask, and I'll come running!'

'An ale and a hot meal whilst sat in a quiet corner of your common room would be most welcome.'

Farley spread his arms. 'Of course, good sir knight,' he said, dashing out from behind the counter. 'Let me help you up to your room.' The innkeeper's scrawny arms were nearly pulled from their sockets under the weight of the knight's helmet.

Sir Lancelot bent low to relieve Farley of his burden. 'Please, do not worry yourself, Master Butterman. You are a busy man.'

'As you wish, sir. I'll not come between a knight and his arms. I'll have a comfortable seat ready for you once you've settled into your lodgings.'

'Most kind, thank you.'

Sir Lancelot mounted the creaking staircase and made his way upstairs. Despite Farley Butterman's claims, the accommodation was small and sparsely furnished. Nonetheless, it was comfortable and more than adequate for a man who spent the majority of his evenings sleeping beneath the stars. He dumped his possessions upon a cot positioned against the wall. Above the bed, a shuttered window—in need of repair—looked out over the stables. *At least I can keep an eye on Cedric.* The innkeeper's boy did not inspire confidence.

A wardrobe occupied the space behind the door, and there was a lockable chest beside. Sir Lancelot secured his helmet and provisions within. Then, too big for the chest, he slid his black shield underneath the cot. For a moment, he was tempted to collapse onto the bed and let sleep take him, but his need to quench his thirst and fill his belly persuaded him otherwise. He made to leave but caught sight of his reflection. A plate of polished tin hung from the wall above a pedestal and basin. *No wonder I scared Farley's boy,* he thought, studying the dishevelled stranger staring back at him.

Dark curling locks hung untamed and unkempt below his shoulders, and a great bushy beard erupted from his jawline, tumbling to his chest like a tangled bush. Yet even though his appearance was changed beyond recognition, his eyes remained the same—dark and knowing. *The eyes of a traitor.* Sir Lancelot sighed. He did not enjoy seeing himself. It reminded him of who he was and what he had become. *And now I have no choice but to confront my demons.* He prayed Guinevere lived and vowed to fetch her to safety no matter the cost to his soul. He tore his gaze from the mirror, consumed with self-loathing and traitorous thoughts.

Filling the basin with a water pitcher, Sir Lancelot submerged his face into the liquid's cool embrace. He would do his duty. He would deliver the queen to his king and slip once more into exile. As a Knight of the Round Table, he would continue devoting his life to the order's cause. He would hunt and rid the lands of Albion of the demon scourge threatening to overrun it.

Sir Lancelot unclasped the heavy cloak from his shoulders, hooking the saturated garment behind the door. Then he unbuckled and removed his assorted items of armour—his mail shirt and splints, his iron-plated greaves and gauntlets—until he stood in nothing but black leather and boots.

Sir Lancelot pulled his wild locks from his face, gathering and securing the hair behind his head in a loose knot. His beard he wove into a plait of sorts. Yet without oil or treatment, it was rough and ill-defined. Nonetheless, Sir Lancelot almost felt human again, and with Secace sheathed and belted at his side, he sought the comforts of the Tipsy Squire's common room.

Chapter Nine

The Peacock & the Wolf

Jovial voices and bouts of merry laughter filled the common room. A fire blazed in the hearth, and lanterns hung from the rafters. The ambience was warm and welcoming, the light mellow, the scene half-veiled in a smoky haze.

Sir Lancelot stooped beneath the knotted beams and made his way between a throng of revellers congregating at the elongated bar. Here, low benches and long tables were populated with heavy drinkers and famished feeders. The smells of roasted meat, fresh-baked bread, and hearty broth were heaven to a hungry soul, and, by Bran's beard, none were hungrier than Sir Lancelot.

Moving through the bar, Sir Lancelot drew many a curious glance. He was a striking man, dark and brooding. And even haggard and travel-worn as he was, he cut an imposing figure. Oozing self-assurance, his every stride was graceful and fluid. He was tall, lean, and strong—a warrior born. All who looked upon him knew it. He was a wolf among sheep.

Beyond the crowded bar and its merrymakers was a quieter space. The chairs here attracted older, wiser occupants—pipe smokers, wine drinkers, profound thinkers, and deep sleepers. Sir Lancelot found himself a suitably dark and secluded corner among them and sunk into the comforts of a well-cushioned armchair. Resting his weary head against the high-backed seat, he closed his eyes, allowing himself a moment's peace. The sounds and smells of the inn were a comfort to Sir Lancelot, a reassuring reminder of the benefits of companionship. He often forgot what it was like being among others, to be among friends and loved ones.

It wasn't long before Sir Lancelot's thoughts dwelt on times past, as they frequently did when his mind wandered. He remembered his life at Camelot with fondness. *I knew such love and camaraderie.* The Knights of the Round Table, brothers to a man, and Sir Lancelot, their champion! Such heady days. Yet now they were over, sacrificed for the love of Guinevere, for the love of his best friend's wife. Arthur deserved better, and Sir Lancelot deserved his fate. Life was cruel.

'Ah, there you are, Sir Galaad,' came the voice of Farley Butterman.

Startled from his trance, Sir Lancelot jerked upright, his right hand finding the hilt of Secace.

'I beg your pardon, sir. I did not mean to disturb you,' Farley apologised. 'Not so abruptly, at any rate.' The knight's sudden response had the man's heart racing well in excess of anything it was accustomed to. How the tray cradled across his arms had not crashed to the boards was a wonder. 'I have brought your supper.'

With shaking hands, the innkeeper placed the tray beside the knight on a small, circular table. 'Bread, cheese, meats—and ale, of course!'

Sir Lancelot nodded his thanks. 'Much obliged, Master Butterman.'

Farley smiled. 'If there is anything else I can do for you, just holler.' The flustered innkeeper hurried away to the bar, where a growing crowd of thirsty customers jostled for position.

Sir Lancelot reached for the ale, draining half the tankard's contents in a single draught. *By Merlin's staff, that hits the mark!* A good ale was hard to come by, not that Sir Lancelot would have cared if the Tipsy Squire's offering was only half so good. From the wooden tray, he tore a chunk of bread from a knotted loaf. It was still warm from the oven. Sir Lancelot greedily devoured the rest and everything else besides. After finishing, he clasped his tankard contentedly and sank once more into the chair's comfortable depths.

To entertain himself before turning in for the night, Sir Lancelot studied the Tipsy Squire's patrons. Determining a man's character by only his appearance and the way in which he carried himself was the task. It was guesswork, but Sir Lancelot was seldom far from the mark.

On the quieter side of the common room, where Sir Lancelot and a good many besides took their rest, sat a young man. Hugging a bottle of something strong, he hunched forward in his chair with a faraway expression etched on a troubled face.

Sir Lancelot examined the man further. His clothes were fine and tailored, his boots spotless and freshly waxed, his fair hair styled and well-presented. Unless he was born into nobility, these niceties were beyond the means of most. And if he was a man of wealth, it beggared the question as to why he chose to drink in the Tipsy Squire. Why not at the castle? Or at one of the more reputable taverns of Astolat, of which there were many.

Sir Lancelot supped his ale, his dark eyes scrutinising his target's every detail. No, this young man was a stranger to wealth—the boots, the finery, the sword at his side… all less than a day or two old. Sir Lancelot shook his head with sadness. *An evil deed will forever sit heavily upon the shoulders of a good man.* The youth's newfound wealth had come at a price; Sir Lancelot could see it in the young man's tormented eyes, and now he faced his demons.

We must all face the consequences of our actions, Sir Lancelot mused sombrely. He understood the truth of his words better than most. The young man would require resolve and inner strength to prevail, and Sir Lancelot wished him well—although, from experience, he knew the bottle gripped in the youth's hands would offer him no solace, only a sore head come morning.

Leaving the youngster to his demons, Sir Lancelot spied an intriguing character at the bar. Grey-haired and mature of age, the man perched atop a stool enjoying a tankard of ale and pipe of weed. At once, Sir Lancelot guessed he was a military man. Cropped hair and clean-shaven, he sat erect and alert with his back against the bar. His face was worn, yet his eyes were keen and always were they watching.

The man eyed a rowdy group of drinkers gathered on the other side of the inn. They were young and proud and full of beer. Sir Lancelot could not see them but could hear them well enough. The rising noise levels in the Tipsy Squire began rivalling those of the Blushing Maiden.

The old soldier carried a sword, but unlike the fair-haired youth, whose blade Sir Lancelot noted was all elaborate scabbard and fancy handguard, the veteran's was plain and simple. Not an overpriced showpiece but a workman's tool, well used and trusted to do a job.

Sir Lancelot suspected he would find a shirt of mail beneath the man's roughspun woollens. Sir Lancelot smiled. Once a soldier, always a soldier. Doubtless, he was a veteran of many a battle, and by his age, battles fought in a time before Arthur and his brave new world—hard battles, bloody battles.

The veteran caught Sir Lancelot's eye, and the pair exchanged a respectful nod, warrior to warrior. *I wager that the old man and his blade have seen more action than all the drunken peacocks with their pretty little play swords combined.* Sir Lancelot was tempted to join him for an ale or two at the bar. He rather fancied the old soldier had a tale to tell. *He might prove a valuable source of information and may know a thing or two about my mystery knight.*

On this occasion, Sir Lancelot's desire to maintain discretion and a clear head outweighed his thirst for knowledge and ale. Tonight, he needed to rest. His search for the witch's scarred brute would begin on the morrow.

Ready for his bed, Sir Lancelot set about draining his tankard. While he did so, the common room erupted with an awful din. A second rowdy group had entered the inn, adding their drunken vocals to the pot.

It seemed the Tipsy Squire was living up to its name. *And no better than the Blushing Maiden, after all,* Sir Lancelot mused, pushing himself to his feet. *It seems I have a busy day ahead of me on the morrow, hunting scarred brutes and new lodgings, too.*

'Well, roast my parsnips! If it is none other than the Black Knight of Corbyn, as I live and breathe!'

Oh, have mercy. Dejected, Sir Lancelot slumped back into his chair as the ruddy, round face of Gaston le Grece beamed at him. The minstrel swayed toward Sir Lancelot on unsteady legs, sploshing red wine from his goblet.

Swiftly, Sir Lancelot stood again. It was apparent the inebriated bard was intent on embracing him come what may, and Sir Lancelot decided it preferable to experience the impending ordeal standing rather than sitting. 'Greetings, Gas—' The knight's breath was squeezed from his lungs by the minstrel's crushing bear hug.

'So, you came after all,' Gaston slurred, grinning like only a drunk can. He held on to Sir Lancelot more for support than affection. The man's red, bulbous nose loomed perilously close, and Sir Lancelot felt the drunk's warm, fetid breath tickle his face.

'Come, let me brandish you with an ale,' the portly poet declared. Leaving Sir Lancelot, he staggered toward the bar and blundered straight into his faithful companions. Pendle and Grenn caught Gaston before he fell, and all without spilling a single drop of wine.

'My friends, see who it is!' Gaston spun around and thrust his goblet at Sir Lancelot. 'None other than our fine friend from the forest!'

The minstrels gathered to greet Sir Lancelot, and all hugged him as Gaston had.

'I am to bed,' Sir Lancelot protested, but the minstrels would have none of it.

'To bed?' Gaston questioned with an exaggerated wink. 'I see no buxom wench to tempt you upstairs?' he added, roaring with laughter.

Before Sir Lancelot could argue his case, a fresh tankard of ale was thrust into his empty hands.

'Let us perform our new ditty for our illustrious friend,' Foggy suggested gleefully.

Sir Lancelot's heart sank. *So much for getting an early night and keeping a low profile.* Resigned to his fate, he once more eased himself into the armchair. Taking a deep draught of ale, he sighed.

He had the feeling it was going to be a long night. *I shall live to regret this.*

Gaston le Grece and the Minstrels of Knoberton brought forth their many instruments, and they began to play:

> *'The fair and lusty maidens of Corbyn,*
> *Stood blonde and busty and all a gawpin'.*
>
> *They stared not in fright at the dreadful wyrm's ferocity,*
> *Yet rather at the sight of the Black Knight's monstrosity.*
>
> *Long and mighty, his weapon did smite the foul monster,*
> *Coy and flirty, the maidens dreamt of a four-poster.*
>
> *Against all the odds, the fearsome Black Knight finally prevailed,*
> *Cursing all the gods, the lonesome maidens had their hopes*
> *curtailed.'*

A second verse followed the first and a third after the second, and each was ruder than the last.

As the minstrels' song ended, those who had gathered to watch—most, if not all, of the Tipsy Squire's patrons—burst into raucous cheer. And now the ditty was over, all eyes turned to its recipient.

Sir Lancelot cringed with discomfort. 'An entertaining performance,' he managed. 'If somewhat fanciful.'

Gaston chortled wholeheartedly. 'Indeed, but what is a story without a little fancy? Dull, that is what it is! And unless our cups are empty, seldom are the Minstrels of Knoberton dull.'

The Black Knight was drawing interest. The fair-haired youth had put aside his demons to stare open-mouthed, and the rowdy revellers from the far side of the bar jeered and pointed. Even the wily old veteran perched atop his stall turned to raise a curious eyebrow.

The Black Knight's deeds were many, and it was rare to see the renowned demon slayer in the flesh. Yet, as ever, when a figure of repute is met, they are more often than not deemed less than the reputation that precedes them.

'*You* are the Black Knight?' a young knight queried, emerging from the throng. He and his friends had ventured from the bar to see the legendary hero for themselves. All were drunk as lords and as disrespectful as knaves. The young man strutted toward Sir Lancelot as arrogantly as a peacock with feathers spread.

Sir Lancelot nodded. 'I am.'

The brazen knight presented himself before Sir Lancelot as if he were heir to Arthur's throne. 'I was under the assumption that the Black Knight was a man of honour—a legend.' He peered down and sneered. 'Not, well, whatever you are, *sir*.'

Sir Lancelot sighed. He had no time for the impertinence of youth, especially not for one so ill-disciplined and aloof. 'Go home to your mother, boy, before I teach you a lesson in manners.'

The young knight was stung by the rebuke, and his party of drunken friends—if friends they were—goaded him into a response. 'You cannot allow this imposter to insult you so, Sir Roderick.'

While the peacock and his entourage plotted amongst themselves, the remainder of the inn's occupants sniggered behind their backs. Even the old veteran cracked a smile. The proud peacock seemed unaccustomed to reprimands, and finding himself the butt of the joke only added to his rising anger.

Flaring his nostrils and puckering his lips, the petulant redhead swung to face Sir Lancelot, 'It is I who shall teach you, Sir Vagabond. I demand an apology, or else I shall demand satisfaction.'

The peacock knight's comrades cheered his words, 'Well said, Sir Roderick. Well said, indeed!' Then, bursting with bravado, Sir Roderick drew his blade and began swishing the thing through the inn's smoky air. 'I wait for your answer, sir.'

Sir Lancelot began to lose patience. For the good of the realm, he had fought and slain more men and monsters than he cared to remember. Yet this insulant whelp demanded an apology for a scolding he well deserved. It required all Sir Lancelot's resolve not to skewer the brat where he stood and be done with it, and if not bound by the knight's code, he may well have done.

Swiftly, seeing how the Black Knight's blood boiled, the old veteran slid from his barstool to intervene, pushing between the pair. He rested a staying hand on Sir Roderick's shoulder. 'Don't do something you'll regret, lad,' he whispered sincerely. 'It'll be best for everyone if you go home and sleep off your ale.'

Sneering contemptuously, Sir Roderick shrugged the veteran's hand away. 'I need no advice from the likes of you, old man,' he said before parading in front of his supporters. 'See how the Black Knight uses others to fight his battles for him—even old-timers! Not such a hero, after all, hey?'

The baying and laughing stopped, and all eyes stared past the strutting peacock.

Slowly, Sir Roderick turned. The imposter had vacated his seat. Sir Roderick gulped. The man in black was much taller than he had expected and broader, too. Fear gripped Sir Roderick's heart. There was something about the man's presence—a deadly confidence he had not felt before. Yet he could not back down, not now, not in front of the men. Fear of humiliation drove the red-haired youngster to act, and he lunged at the Black Knight with his longsword.

'No!' the veteran bellowed, watching Sir Roderick's glinting blade arrow toward Sir Lancelot's heart as if in slow motion.

Time seemed to speed up once more, and in the blink of an eye, the Black Knight sidestepped the peacock's clumsy thrust and, with a well-placed boot to the youth's bony rear, dispatched him headlong into the vacant armchair behind him.

The Tipsy Squire exploded with fresh laughter.

Sir Roderick gathered himself. He was far from done. Maddened by rage, he leapt at Sir Lancelot, hacking with his sword again and again.

The Black Knight swayed left and right, evading the peacock's every move with effortless ease, the crowd cheering and jeering louder and louder with each misplaced blow.

Proceedings became serious when Sir Roderick encouraged his comrades into the fray, 'What are you waiting for? Help me!' A dozen swords hissed into the air, and Sir Roderick backed himself into their protection. 'Not so sure of yourself now, are you, Sir Vagabond!'

Sir Lancelot pulled Secace from his scabbard. Once more, the inn was silenced. The Black Knight's blade shone brighter than the fire blazing in the hearth, yet not with an orange light, but a shining silver to dazzle the eyes.

To Sir Lancelot's surprise, the veteran had come with sword in hand to stand at his side. 'Edgar,' said the man in the way of an introduction. And then, the blond-haired youth joined him, too. 'Percy at your service,' he announced, drawing his fancy blade.

The Tipsy Squire's innkeeper, resembling a man who was but one stressful situation away from heart failure, appeared between the combatants, flailing his sweaty hands above his head in panic. 'Withdraw your blades, good sirs! This is a tavern, not the battlefield. I beg you, wait for the tourney!' The poor man was flustered beyond measure.

To ease the tension, Gaston and his merry minstrels took up their instruments for a second time and, joining the beleaguered innkeeper, relieved the taunt atmosphere with a cheerful ditty.

Sir Roderick and his comrades sheathed their weapons. 'Do you fight on the morrow?' the peacock called behind Farley Butterman and the bards.

'I do,' Sir Lancelot answered. Sir Roderick's insolence had stirred the Black Knight into action. *And besides*, he told himself, *taking part in the tournament will grant me access to the competitors.* And what better way to find Hellawes' scarred knight than as a contender.

'Then I shall see you on the field,' Sir Roderick promised scornfully before he and his friends slunk away into the night.

Feeling generous, a thankful Farley Butterman lined the bar with tankards, and the night swiftly unravelled into an ale-induced blur of drunken merriment. By evening's end, all Astolat knew of the Black Knight's arrival and his intentions to become the tournament's champion.

Chapter Ten

Into Battle

The Black Knight's brief time at the Tipsy Squire was at an end, much to Farley Butterman's regret. Having a figure of repute lodging at his inn was good for business. Although, if last night's shenanigans were anything to go by, perhaps the Tipsy Squire was better off without the knight's custom. Stress and Farley Butterman's heart were not a sustainable match.

At first light, Sir Lancelot set his new companions to work, sending Edgar to enter his name into the lists and Percy to acquire a contestant's pavilion out on the meadow.

After a last breakfast at the inn—a full plate of bacon and eggs to settle his sour belly and a tall pitcher of chilled rosewater to soothe his thumping head—Sir Lancelot set off to find a reputable blacksmith. He nor his steed were equipped to compete in a tournament unless they were prepared to endure more than their fair share of misery.

Astolat boasted an abundance of forges to choose from, but in matters of warfare, Sir Lancelot only used the best, and by all accounts, Bergan was his man.

'I have scarce enough to offer you, sir knight,' Bergan declared. 'If only you had sought my services a week or two past, then yes, my wares were plentiful. Alas, as you can see, now not so.'

Sir Lancelot cast his eyes about the blacksmith's forge. The place was all but barren. Three dusty helmets lined a high shelf, a solitary shirt of mail hung from a wooden mannequin on display by the window, a mix of swords rested point-first inside an iron scuttle, and a large tin drum contained a meagre offering of greaves, gauntlets, and odds and ends. Nonetheless, what remained was of the highest workmanship.

'Perchance a smith of your standing might have the qualities to enhance what I already have?'

'Well, yes, that might be the case, but there is little time before you'll be needing such enhancements.' The burly blacksmith eyed Sir Lancelot sideways, making no effort to conceal his scepticism. 'And, if truth be told, I'll wager my skills will be in high demand once the day is done. There'll be no shortage of knights wearing dents and gashes and all needing bending and rendering. And by the look of it, I'm guessing they'll pay more than you.' He shrugged his broad shoulders apologetically. 'No offence, sir knight.'

Despite his fragile state, Sir Lancelot chuckled. He admired the man's honesty, if not his greed. Untying a cord from his leathers, the knight tossed a small pouch at the smithy. 'Looks can be deceiving,' he said. 'I think you will find sufficient coin to hire your services for the duration of the tournament.'

After pulling open the pouch, Bergan's eyes lit up. 'Indeed, good sir knight!' Abruptly, the big man spun to peer into the gloomy depths of the building. 'Jasper!' Bergan's young, bare-chested apprentice was pumping on the bellows, building up the furnace in readiness for the day ahead. 'Jasper! Come, boy, let us be about our work. We have much to do!'

Bergan and his apprentice worked miracles within the short time before the tournament began. In addition to Cedric's hardened leather coat, the horse's flanks were further protected with a smattering of mail and his head with an iron-plated shaffron. Also, the smith modified Sir Lancelot's saddle so he might better absorb a glancing blow. As for Sir Lancelot himself, he was furnished with iron-plated thigh and shoulder guards and a breastplate, too. The amour was heavier than Sir Lancelot was accustomed to and thicker than his mail and splint. *It is crude, yet against a lance strike, it will more than prove its worth.* Bergan was a man ahead of his time.

Edgar and Percy acquired the services of a seamstress at Astolat's market, and Cedric was duly adorned in a new black livery and his master in a matching black surcoat to be worn over his leather, mail, and plate. When Sir Lancelot made his way to Astolat's fields, never had he appeared more like his alter ego, the Black Knight.

Cedric's hooves clipped and clopped through the bustling streets. Edgar and Percy walked beside horse and rider, both overcome by the volume of excited support lining the way, all of which were eager to glimpse the legendary Black Knight before the tournament began. Astride Cedric's back, Sir Lancelot did not share their excitement. The ill-effects of the previous night's antics had yet to dissipate, and in the cold light of day, there was much to regret—a sore head was the least of his worries.

The night had been long, and the ale free-flowing. At the peak of merriment, the Tipsy Squire surpassed the Blushing Maiden as Astolat's rowdiest tavern. By evening's end, after many a song was sung, dance danced, tale told, and drink drunk, the Black Knight had gained a squire, a sword brother, and a lover—the last of which he lamented with all his heart. *Now, I have betrayed Guinevere as well as Arthur.* What sort of knight was he? *No knight at all, only a breaker of oaths.*

Late in the night, after Sir Lancelot had finally fallen into his cot in a state of delirium, he had been awoken by an unexpected visitor. Concealed within the depths of cloak and cowl, Elayne the Fair had come uninvited to Sir Lancelot's lodgings. News of the Black Knight's arrival had spread like the pox, even, it appeared, as far as the castle.

Come morning, young Percy believed redemption was to be found in the service of Sir Galaad le Noir. After all, every knight needed a squire. Edgar once fought for a king and would now follow a knight. The veteran pledged to watch the Black Knight's back for the likes of Sir Roderick. Once a soldier, always a soldier. And as for Elayne the Fair, Sir Lancelot had given her something he really ought not to have done. Although, in his defence, the woman had offered him little opportunity to decline her advances. What man could? Bewitched by Elayne's beauty, Sir Lancelot had pledged his sword to her father's cause and, while under the befuddling influence of ale and wine, his undying love for his daughter.

The Great Melee was a two-day spectacle. For the most part, the contest was a dramatic means to cull the field before the jousting began and was the nearest experience most folk were ever likely to get to a real battle. The people loved it. To witness two hundred armour-clad knights doing their utmost to unhorse one another was a sight to behold and not for the fainthearted. Over the years, the crowds of Astolat had seen many a knight lose their lives in some brutal way or another and many more their wits.

Reaching the field, Sir Lancelot saw a myriad of banners flying above the stands and in the meadows. He shook his head with sadness. *So many are here when they ought to be standing with their king.* And he included himself among them. *Or, at the very least, searching the land for their queen. The kings of Albion grow complacent.*

The marshal of the games—a stout, red-faced man bedecked in tournament finery—held a shining trumpet to his lips. A blaring blast followed, peeling over the crowded stands and surrounding fields.

Draped in stately robes of blue, Lord Astolat stood. 'Eat, drink, and spend money!' he declared in a booming voice. 'And above all, enjoy the tournament!'

Once again, the marshal's horn echoed through Astolat. The tournament was officially underway.

As was tradition, the competitors paraded before the people under the banners and colours of their houses and liege lords. Firstly, the knights passed the stands where Astolat's aristocrats watched from their seats. Then, traversing the field's extremities, the knights performed a lap of honour for the benefit of those folk ringing the perimeter.

The marshal announced the knights of repute. In pride of place and first to parade before the excited audience was none other than King Arthur's greatest warrior, Sir Gawain, knight of the Round Table. The noble warrior waved to his cheering fans astride a mighty grey charger, Arthur Pendragon's roaring red dragon banner fluttering atop the knight's hoisted lance.

Arthur sends his best man, Sir Lancelot mused. Was Sir Gawain here for glory? Or was he at Astolat for the same reason as Sir Lancelot? Had Arthur dispatched his greatest knight to find his queen?

A lengthy line of knights followed in Sir Gawain's wake. Once the Pendragon banner had been raised, lords, knights, and freelancers flocked to the hero's side. After them came the knights of Lyonesse, Cameliard, Tintagel, Logres, Gore, Ratae, and many more, their numerous crests colouring the parade.

'King Borticus of Badon!' the marshal of the games called. 'Sir Blamor de Gallis!' The competing knights rode before the terraces bare-faced, their helmets hooked over their saddles. The march was a procession of square jaws, dimpled chins, manicured manes, and well-groomed beards. But not Sir Lancelot. The Black Knight rode with his helmet firmly in place, his identity hidden beneath. The field was full of familiar faces, and there were some who might recognise the exiled knight despite his overgrown beard and wild locks.

'Sir Galaad le Noir!' The crowds rejoiced as if the herald had introduced King Arthur himself, or at least Sir Lancelot and not his pretend counterpart. Amongst the stands, the maidens and ladies of Astolat hustled and bustled for the right to bestow their favours. No knight sent more ladies clambering for his attention than Sir Galaad le Noir, not even the esteemed Sir Gawain.

Spotting Lady Elayne amidst the writhing masses, Sir Lancelot lowered his black lance so she might slide her favour around the blunted tip of his weapon. Dipping his head in acknowledgement, the Black Knight kicked Cedric on. 'Good luck!' he heard Percy call. Beneath his helmet, Sir Lancelot grinned. He seldom had need of luck in battle.

Stationed upon the frosted field alongside King Pelles' men, Sir Lancelot tied Elayne's favour around his helmet—bright scarlet on black.

'You carry my sister's colours well, Sir Galaad,' observed Sir Lavaine, Lady Elayne's brother and son of King Pelles.

Sir Lancelot nodded but did not reply. The knight busied himself by scanning the field for signs of Hellawes' scarred brute.

A needle in a haystack, he decided with a resigned sigh. Instead, he watched Sir Gawain encourage his men. The knight of the Round Table shone as brightly as the morning sun. His polished scale gleamed like a sea serpent, beautiful and elegant. Sir Gawain wheeled his mount about, offering tactics and wisdom to his supporters. *I wish I were fighting at Sir Gawain's side once more*, Sir Lancelot mused. Yet, he only had himself to blame.

Twisting in his saddle, Sir Lancelot faced Sir Lavaine. 'Keep with me,' he said. 'Refrain from attempting anything rash. Leave heroics for the later rounds.'

The field was set, the tournament of Astolat ready. It was time for the Great Melee.

Chapter Eleven

The Great Melee

The low winter sun shone brightly, glinting from the field of metal men. Beneath their barded steeds, the frosted grass of the meadow glistened white.

Sir Lancelot knocked the visor of his helmet closed, wincing as the face guard clanged into position. His skull ached abominably, and the smell of his own rank breath turned his stomach. Stale mead was all he could taste. Sir Lancelot was unused to drinking, at least in such quantities as was consumed the previous night. His head banged like a battle drum, and his belly churned and bubbled like a witch's cauldron. *Gaston and his minstrels have much to answer for.*

At least the weather had improved. Overnight, the bitter north wind had pushed the sleet and snow south to leave clear skies above, and now the tournament fields of Astolat sparkled like a frozen lake.

Sir Lancelot gulped down great big lungfuls of ice-cold winter air. *I will need more than fresh air to clear my head,* he thought ruefully. Yet the prospect of battle sharpened his mind. Stirring to his task, Sir Lancelot studied the field. Those fighting for the northern kings, Loarn and Lot, had combined their strength.

'Do you see how King Pellinor's men are keen to meet the Northmen head-on?' Sir Lancelot said to Sir Lavaine. King Pellinor of Listenoise, Sir Lavaine's uncle, shared a blood feud with King Lot of Lothian. In truth, most kings shared a blood feud with King Lot.

'Should we not ally ourselves to my uncle's forces?' Sir Lavaine questioned. He eyed the menacing northern contingent with a troubled frown. They rode their mounts bare-faced, some bare-chested, and each streaked with blue woad. Forsaking armour was a show of bravado but ill-advised. Even a blunted lance could kill. Nonetheless, they were fearsome to behold.

'Mayhap,' Sir Lancelot answered. 'It would be an honourable cause, would it not? Alas, to advance into the latter stages of the tourney, we must use our wits as well as our brawn.' Sir Lancelot shifted his gaze, nodding toward the western kings, Einion and Ceredig. 'The sunburst and Annwn's hounds will fight none save for the Pendragon, and my guess is King Nath's eagle will add to Sir Gawain's plight. Tournaments are ever political.' King Nath hailed from the Emerald Isle, and he and his kin hungered for Albion and her riches.

Sir Lavaine spied Lord Vortimer, 'See yonder, yet another adversary for the high king's knights.'

Vortimer's father, Vortigern, was himself high king for a brief time. The knave betrayed Arthur's father, Uther Pendragon, conspiring with Saxon warlords to gain the throne. But the new high king had not wagered on young Arthur uniting Albion against him. Vortigern was slain by Arthur himself, and the traitor's Saxon henchmen were sent fleeing into the east.

As a consequence of his father's infamous deeds, the young Vortimer was stripped of land and rank, becoming a nameless knight, nothing more than a freelancer. Be that as it may, the crown's enemies were quick to offer their support, and here at

Astolat, there was no shortage of knights massed beneath the renegade's banner.

'The fanged serpent,' Sir Lancelot observed. 'A fitting coat-of-arms for a viperous bloodline.'

King Bagdemagus of the western borders—ever a thorn in the side of the Pendragon—had joined the serpent, his banner of three grey watchtowers on a field of green fluttering in the wind. *Another foe for Sir Gawain to face*, Sir Lancelot thought. Yet such was Lord Vortimer's nature that he and his allies were likely to avoid sterner confrontations in favour of weaker quarry.

'We will need to be wary of the likes of Vortimer,' Sir Lancelot warned. 'He seldom chances his hand against the might of the banner kings—Pendragon, Logres, Lyonesse, Caerleon, Camelilard, and the like. He will prey on the lesser kings and lords in their stead, and I count our ranks among them.'

Cedric tossed his head with impatience. Flaring his nostrils, the animal snorted misted breath into the air. He could smell the impending contest, sense it coming like scent on the breeze. A seasoned warhorse was worth its weight in gold on the battlefield, and there was none wiser in war than Cedric.

Sir Lancelot calmed his mount, patting the animal's flank reassuringly. In the absence of companionship during his years of lonely exile, Cedric had become a dear friend.

'We must be canny. Defend if we are singled out and commit ourselves only when an ally is in dire need. It may only be a tournament, but as ever, there is more riding on its outcome than meets the eye. Concentrate your efforts on the Charge of Seven Kings. Once safely negotiated, we shall see how the land lies.'

A short blast from the marshal's horn heightened the tension. The crowds encircling the field and watching from the stands roared with anticipation. Discontented jackdaws perched amongst the treetops spread their black wings before cawing into the skies.

Above the bobbing heads of Astolat's spectators, flags of support waved back and forth—the dragon, the phoenix, the rose, the falcon, the hammer, the boar, the crossed swords, the wolf, the grail, the lightning rod, and the rearing stallion. Youngsters straddled their father's shoulders, staring wide-eyed with excitement; maidens gazed longingly at the gallant knights with galloping hearts, and old-timers peered through blurry eyes with rueful regret of what once was.

The stage was set, and the horn was blown. The Great Melee was begun.

At once, the rumbling of hooves thundered over the field, a pounding cacophony shaking the earth like an earthquake. Clods of frosted grass and frozen mud flew into the cold winter air torn from the ground. Gathering pace, the warhorses powered across the meadow, their breath a swirling fog.

Atop their mighty beasts, the knights of Albion lowered their lances and braced themselves for contact. The staring crowds held their breath, thrilled, horrified, and enthralled. Some turned their heads, some grinned in sheer wonderment, and some paled with worry and strife.

Like two midsummer storms colliding, the knights met. Lances whistled past plumed helmets, glanced from iron-plated shoulder guards, punched into mail-clad bodies, and shattered against shields of linden. The noise was deafening. Man and mount crashed together. The audience 'oohed' as knights were knocked from their saddles and 'aahed' as others clung on for dear life. The children perched high on their father's shoulders covered their eyes while the maidens with galloping hearts swooned left, right, and centre as men began littering the meadow like autumn leaves.

The Great Melee began with the Charge of Seven Kings, and its origins hark from an age long since forgotten. Before Roman galleys arrived upon the shores of Albion, legend tells of a valiant but tragic tale.

Seven kings held sway over the land, but each grew disgruntled with the other's rule. After countless years of feuding, the kings decided to settle their grievances once and for all. Upon the field of battle, the seven kings and their seven armies faced one another. Not knowing which of their enemies to vanquish before the other, the kings charged forth as one, and when after seven days and seven nights, the conflict was at an end, none yet lived.

It was likely the story was born in a tavern and nurtured by drunks and bards and was nothing more than a fanciful tale. Yet seldom is there smoke without fire.

Emerging from the Charge of Seven Kings unscathed, Sir Lancelot wheeled Cedric alongside Sir Lavaine, 'Well jousted, sir.'

Sir Lancelot had swept a knight in green from his horse, an eagle of King Nath, and Sir Lavaine, a man of Badon, but King Pelles had lost men too.

Sir Lancelot pointed his black lance toward a small grove of elm, their bare branches overhanging the field at its furthest extremity, far from the stands and cheering spectators. 'Let us regroup beneath the trees yonder.'

'Agreed.' Sir Lavaine answered, raising his lance so his knights might see. 'King Pelles!' he called. 'On me!'

Sir Lancelot and Sir Lavaine led the white and gold knights across the meadow, King Pelles' flaming phoenix flying from their lances. Behind them boomed another mighty crash. A good number of riders had charged for a second time and then, with a less audible outcome, a third. These were knights seeking fame and fortune. Many a reputation was built on such foolhardy daring, not least long ago, Sir Lancelot's and Sir Gawain's.

Arriving beneath the elm, King Pelles' knights swung their mounts to survey the scene. The mass of combatants slowly disentangled themselves from the fray and, just as King Pelles' men had done, rallied beneath their banners, leaving behind a scattering of unhorsed knights upon the frozen field. Most trudged dejectedly from the meadow and the contest, but an unfortunate few remained unmoving. Sir Lancelot and Sir Lavaine watched teams driving horse-drawn carts recover the bodies before carrying them from the meadow.

While the last of the maimed withdrew to safety, the alliance of three kings—eagle, hound, and sunburst—mobilised their forces into position. 'As I thought,' Sir Lancelot spoke. 'The Emerald Isle takes sides with the western kings. And look,' he directed Sir Lavaine's gaze easterly, 'they challenge the Pendragon.'

'And there,' Sir Lavaine announced, 'King Pellinor's men take to the field!'

Sir Lancelot nodded. 'And there is no surprise to whom they seek in combat—King Lot's brood.'

Yet now, Sir Lancelot and Sir Lavaine had concerns of their own to contend with. Just as the Black Knight had feared, the fanged serpent was moving against them. Lord Vortimer and his black-clad henchmen had slithered forth to stalk easy game. The white snake was joined by King Bagdemagus' grey and green watchtowers, and under their combined banners, they drew near.

'Ready your knights, Sir Lavaine,' Sir Lancelot advised. 'In my experience, the best form of defence is attack. Are you with me?'

Sir Lavaine grinned beneath his helmet. 'I am with you!' Excitement coursed through his veins. To ride into battle alongside the Black Knight against none other than the viperous Lord Vortimer was what dreams were made of. *Lesser deeds have been immortalised by bards and minstrels in the halls of kings!*

'Come then, follow my lead!' Sir Lancelot called, digging his heels into Cedric's flanks.

'I thought you said heroics were for the latter stages?' Sir Lavaine yelled. With heart hammering and blood pumping, the young knight kicked his mount into a gallop.

The white and gold knights formed the wings of the phoenix, and at its head rode the Black Knight. The fiery bird smashed into its prey, cleaving into the shadowed heart of Lord Vortimer's army. Yet the black-clad snakes were many, and now the grey and green knights of King Bagdemagus, led by a giant on a mighty midnight charger, thundered to the aid of the fanged serpent.

Dispatching a viper to the dirt, Sir Lancelot swung Cedric to meet the new danger. 'On Cedric, on!' he cried, surging across the meadow with Sir Lavaine at his side. Lowering his lance, he pounded straight at their leader—the giant bull-helmeted brute.

The pair collided with a tremendous crash, both riders rocking in their saddles, their lances shattering against one another's shields.

Swiftly, Sir Lancelot discarded his ruined lance and drew his blunted sword. But before the contest progressed, their paths drifted apart, and the giant knight disappeared into the writhing pack of bodies and horses.

Guiding Cedric, Sir Lancelot deflected a lance with his black shield before skillfully slashing his blade across a knight's snake-crested helmet, sending him clattering from his horse.

'Sir Lavaine!' Sir Lancelot called. 'We must withdraw!' Their gallant assault had not sent Lord Vortimer running as hoped. Instead, the nameless lord, buoyed by his ally's stoic resistance to the golden phoenix's charge, began urging his men onto the front foot again.

'Too late, Sir Galaad,' Sir Lavaine replied bleakly. 'The serpent has us trapped, and now the beast constricts its coils!'

'Have faith, sir,' Sir Lancelot said. 'Stick close, fight well, and we may yet win the right to return on the morrow.'

King Pelles' golden knights gathered, uniting in their defence against Lord Vortimer's encircling forces. Once more, Sir Lancelot spotted the giant bull-helmeted knight riding at the forefront of the opposing brood, 'Who leads Bagdemagus' men?'

'The knight's name is Sir Tarquin,' Sir Lavaine answered. 'He is Lord Mellegrans' man.'

Lord Mellegrans was King Bagdemagus' eldest son, and of all his five siblings, he was by far the cruellest and most ambitious.

Sir Tarquin, Sir Lancelot mused. *Why is the name familiar to me?* There was no time to ponder the knight's identity. 'Here they come!'

Those still possessing lances came first. The black-clad knights levelled their weapons at speed, using their momentum to drive their lances into King Pelles' static host. Shields were raised, and blows were blocked, but those without shields or lacking the skill or opportunity to utilise them were punched from their saddles.

'Push forward!' Sir Lancelot bellowed. 'Get inside their reach!'

Sir Lancelot led by example and wedged Cedric alongside a snake. Frantically, the enemy knight tried wielding his weapon, but the lance was cumbersome to employ at close quarters, and he could do nothing to prevent Sir Lancelot's sword from prodding him unceremoniously from his steed.

Many shared the snake's fate. Wheeling his warhorse hither and thither, the Black Knight dispatched a succession of foes to the frozen field and as each of Lord Vortimer's knights hit the ground, the crowds cheered louder and louder.

Sir Lavaine fought at Sir Lancelot's side, awed by the speed and accuracy of the warrior's blade. If not for Lord Vortimer's allies, and especially the giant Sir Tarquin who butchered white and gold knights from their saddles nearly as rapidly and as ruthlessly as Sir Lancelot did black, grey and green, the snake would have surely slithered away to eye easier pickings.

Under the banner of a black boar, King Borticus of Baden joined the melee. And no sooner had King Borticus' knights exchanged blows with Lord Vortimer's did Sir Balmor de Gallis thunder into the fray. The Knights of the Blue Falcon tore into Sir Tarquin's grey and green watchtowers, reducing the corner of the field in which they fought into a writhing sea of chaos.

Amidst the madness of the melee, the Black Knight's name was called, 'Sir Galaad le Noir! I challenge thee!' A knight appeared from the battling multitudes. Emblazoned upon the man's black shield was Lord Vortimer's white serpent.

'Accepted,' Sir Lancelot answered, wheeling Cedric to intercept.

'Do you not desire to know your adversary's name?'

'I care not,' Sir Lancelot replied. 'It is enough to know you fight for the likes of Vortimer.'

All the same, Sir Lancelot's opponent pushed up his helmet's face guard, revealing his identity. 'I am Sir Roderick!' he announced triumphantly. 'And I will have satisfaction, sir!'

From within the depths of his helmet, Sir Lancelot rolled his eyes, and while Sir Roderick fumbled to reposition his face guard, the Black Knight was on him.

In a flash, Sir Roderick's sword was swept from his grasp, and Sir Lancelot's blade was resting on his shoulder. 'As I said, I care not.'

Sir Roderick's face paled, for he understood his fate—a painful and embarrassing union with the turf beneath his horse.

Sir Lancelot drew back his blade, ready to dispatch Sir Roderick into the dirt, but another knight thrust his steed between the pair.

Adorned in fine black livery, gleaming black mail, and a helmet shaped like a snake's head was Lord Vortimer himself, and his sword snapped at the Black Knight like a striking cobra.

Swiftly, Sir Lancelot shifted his shield to deflect the effort, and with Sir Roderick forgotten, their blades met with a resounding clang. Yet, as the two rivals engaged in combat, the sound of the marshal's horn filled the skies. The untimely stop to proceedings was accompanied by a chorus of boos. For today, the Great Melee was at an end.

'We will finish this on the morrow, sir,' Lord Vortimer hissed.

'So be it,' grunted Sir Lancelot in reply.

Chapter Twelve

A Gifted Horse

The crowds of Astolat cheered the knights from the field. The battle-weary riders funnelled past the stands, heading for a well-earned rest and a goblet of ale before returning on the morrow.

Risking a cuff about the head, a half-dozen young boys and girls squeezed between the soldiers lining the ropes. The urchins sought a closer look at their heroes. A daring few touched a warhorse's flank or, if they were brave enough, a knight's scabbard. It was harmless fun. The competitors obliged them amiably, ruffling hair or tossing a coin, but not all were so accommodating.

Fresh from his frustration in the melee, the sullen Sir Roderick was in no mood for charity. An excited youth's enthusiasm was met only with anger—and a gauntleted fist. Sent tumbling, the boy sprawled headfirst in the trodden earth, where he lay snivelling into his sleeves.

It seems I have yet to teach Sir Roderick humility, Sir Lancelot mused. He followed a horse's length behind Lord Vortimer's ill-mannered apprentice and did not take kindly to the runt's actions. *Perchance I can right a wrong and cheer Sir Roderick's victim.*

Reaching down, Sir Lancelot grabbed a handful of the boy's woollen cowl and hauled him into the air. At first, the urchin shrieked in alarm, but once safely deposited in front of Sir Lancelot, his little dirt-smudged face beamed with joy—and after twisting around to see who had pulled him from the mire, his joy was surpassed by euphoria. 'The Black Knight!' he gasped.

The folk of Astolat applauded Sir Lancelot's noble gesture, and they began calling his name, 'The Black Knight! The Black Knight!'

The youth astride Sir Lancelot's warhorse grinned from ear to ear, and the glowing red mark that throbbed upon his cheek was already forgotten.

Soon after, the crowds chanted the name of another knight fresh from the meadow, 'Sir Gawain! Sir Gawain!' The knight of the Round Table had not disappointed during the melee. Sir Gawain and those allied to the high king's dragon banner had scattered the alliance of three kings across the meadow, unhorsing the mighty Sir Niall of the Emerald Isle—King Nath's nephew—for good measure. Elsewhere, Sir Pellinor's Grail Knights had fought the kings Loarn and Lot's blue-faced heathens to a standstill, and Sir Galleron of Lyonesse had got the better of Sir Melyot of Logres.

For those who packed the stands and lined the fields, the morrow promised more of the same. The talk amongst the people was of Sir Gawain's noble deeds and of King Pelles' fighting phoenix and the deadly Black Knight amidst their gallant ranks.

Ponderously, Sir Lancelot fought his way through the masses as they streamed from the arena in their hundreds. Now lacking the protection offered by Lord Astolat's soldiers, he was hustled by merry well-wishers and zealous fanatics.

'Good fortune on the morrow, sir!'

'Will you marry me, good sir? And if not me, then perchance my sister?'

'Join Sir Gawain and smash King Nath back across the sea!'

'Bury the snakes beneath the dirt!'

Finally freeing himself from the mob, Sir Lancelot found Edgar and Percy waiting to escort him to his pavilion.

'Greetings, Sir Galaad,' Percy said. 'Seldom have I seen a knight perform so admirably in the melee! Perhaps, in time, you might consider teaching me your tricks?'

Edgar scoffed. 'Tricks? A knight's lifelong devotion to his calling is no *trick*. It is paid for in cuts and bruises and in blood and sweat.' The veteran shook his head as he helped Sir Lancelot's young passenger from his horse. The boy was still grinning. 'You have much to learn, Percy.'

'Will you teach me, too, Sir Black Knight?' the urchin beseeched even before his feet had touched the ground.

Sir Lancelot chuckled. 'Mayhap,' he said, 'when you are older and wiser.'

Bursting with pride, the youth stood beaming. He could not wait to tell his friends how the Black Knight was going to train him.

Percy smiled fondly. 'He will have a tale to tell,' he said, watching the boy dart away into the crowds.

Percy led Cedric by the reins while Edgar kept the Black Knight's fans at bay. He scowled and glared at any who ventured too near and discouraged the most ardent of well-wishers from Sir Lancelot's path with a staff of twisted birch, which he swished with venom.

Following the River Ast, the three companions passed through bustling streets and lively winter markets. The tournament had breathed new life into Astolat, and now the town was transformed into a hive of activity. Food stalls were everywhere, seemingly risen from the Otherworld overnight. There were smoked meats and hearty pies, seasonal fruits and roasted nuts, honey cakes and sweet bakes, crusted loaves and chunks of cheese. Their wafting smells were finally enough to banish Sir Lancelot's self-inflicted malady and serve as a reminder that he had not filled his belly since the first rays of dawn.

Soon, the river's tranquil waters guided them to the contestant's meadow—or Champion's Meadow as the camp was otherwise known. The Ast wound its way beside the meadow's green grass, and at its most southerly point, its shallow banks were shielded by lines of mature willow trees, their drooping branches overhanging the river.

A pretty place come spring and summer, Sir Lancelot thought. He imagined the trees in leaf and the meadow in flower. *Yet, as ever, winter's rule drains the land, leaving it grey and forlorn.* Nonetheless, with the sun shining overhead and a myriad of brightly coloured pavilions and tents beneath, Champion's Meadow was as vibrant as midsummer's eve.

The larger pavilions commanded the prime riverside location, but no matter in which direction Sir Lancelot swept his gaze, all manner of makeshift abodes covered the campsite. Atop the biggest of them, giant banners rippled in the breeze. Lesser accommodation was not without crest nor colour, the standards flapping from flagpoles, spears, and lances.

Towering above the rest, King Arthur's red dragon dominated the southern quarter. Sir Lancelot spotted the black boar of Baden, the shining grail of Listenoise, the red rose of Lyonesse, the mighty silver hammer of Caerleon, the rearing white stallion of Logres, the crossed swords of Camelilard, the blue falcon of Gore, and, of course, Corbyn's golden phoenix.

Positioned at the furthest edge of the meadow camped King Bagdemagus' men, three grey watchtowers streaming from their pavilions. And beside them, Lord Vortimer's black tents and banners, each adorned with their master's white-fanged serpents.

The knights of the North, the West, and from across the sea—the men of kings, Loarn and Lot, of Einin and Ceredis, and of Nath—had stationed themselves at the fringes of Astolat. Blood feuds and waring neighbours were not good bedfellows. As for Lord Vortimer, he believed it was his right to share the meadow. After all, had his father not served as high king before Arthur? It was no secret the wretch craved Arthur's crown, and all knew how low he would stoop to snatch it from his noble head. All were welcome to compete at Astolat, regardless of allegiances.

The lords and nobles, including Sir Gawain and other knights of prestige, lodged as guests at Lord Astolat's castle. Not for the first time, Sir Lancelot experienced a pang of regret. *A true knight of the Round Table should not allow himself to be distracted by riches or fame.* Sir Lancelot would pay for his sins. *A modest camp beside the river will be more than I deserve.*

'Here we are, Sir Galaad.'

Stirred from his thoughts, Sir Lancelot realised Cedric had halted, and now his horse tossed its mane with apparent impatience. 'Percy, how has my purse stretched so far to afford such as this?' A giant black pavilion topped by a vast black banner eclipsed in size and stature only by the largest of the Pendragon domes and then only by a hairsbreadth, reared before him. A modest camp by the river, this was not.

'Ah, yes, about that,' Percy replied hesitantly. 'As you know, whilst you prepared for the contest, I was sent to acquire a tent here upon the meadow.'

'Yes, Percy, I am well aware of the first part of the story. It is what follows that intrigues me.'

Edgar cracked a smile.

'Yes, well, the strangest thing happened. As I enquired on your behalf regarding such a tent, the marshal's clerk, with whom these bookings must be made—'

'Get on with it, Percy.'

'Well, as soon as I mentioned your good self, he glanced up from his ledger and informed me that he had been expecting you. And, furthermore, your accommodation was ready, waiting, and paid for—but by whom, the clerk did not know or would not say.'

Sir Lancelot returned his gaze to the pavilion. Perchance a gift from King Pelles? But if so, why had the king not conveyed a message via his son, Sir Lavaine, whom Sir Lancelot had spent the afternoon fighting alongside? And if not his son, then surely his daughter, Lady Elayne, who, after the previous night's frivolities, Sir Lancelot knew only too well. *Yet if not King Pelles, then who?* He was Sir Galaad le Noir, the mystery Black Knight, but now it seemed he had a secret benefactor who was as elusive as he.

Edgar sensed Sir Lancelot's uncertainty. 'There is an old truth that my father once used, "Do not look a gift horse in the mouth".'

Percy stared at the veteran with a frown. 'And pray tell, what nonsense is that?'

Sir Lancelot yanked free his helmet. 'It means do not find fault with something freely given,' he said, scratching at his shaggy mane.

'And what does that have to do with a horse's mouth?' Percy said, puzzled by Edgar's adage.

Sir Lancelot sighed. He was promptly reminded why he enjoyed his own company. Explaining ancient proverbs to ill-informed squires was one of many tedious consequences of a life spent with others. 'If you are fortunate enough to be gifted a horse, do not check its teeth to gauge the animal's age and health. Simply accept the gift graciously and without question.'

Edgar nodded his approval. 'Well said, sir.'

'So, you compare the pavilion to a gifted horse?'

'Yes, Percy, there you have it,' Sir Lancelot said. The boy was a slow learner.

'I see,' Percy replied, promptly securing Cedric beneath the pavilion's awning. 'In that case,' he held back the heavy linen curtain covering the entrance, 'after you, sir.'

The pavilion's spacious interior was something to behold, especially for Percy, who was unaccustomed to seeing such splendour. 'Sir Galaad, your camp is fit for a king,' he declared with wonder.

Sir Lancelot found it impossible to disagree. On the outside, the pavilion was as drab as a wet night in Londinium, but colour and intrigue waited within. Sir Lancelot discovered a four-poster bed smothered in thick furs and wrapped with patterned drapes fit for royalty.

Percy was drawn to a bountiful selection of fresh produce strewn across a table. 'None will starve whilst under the Black Knight's roof!'

Edgar stared into a full-length mirror. Captivated, he marvelled at his reflection gleaming right back at him in the polished tin and copper.

Yet hidden beyond a curtain, a smaller area revealed the pavilion's greatest secret. 'Praise be,' Sir Lancelot mouthed in reverence. Upon the pelt of a mighty black bear stood a bath. After a day of hardship and toil, there was no more pleasing sight in all the world. *Except for finding a disrobed Guinevere waiting within.* Sir

Lancelot chased the alluring image from his thoughts. *A knight of the Round Table is pure of heart.*

The tub was fashioned from tin and timber, and soft linen lined the interior to protect sensitive posteriors.

Returning to the others, Sir Lancelot found them as he had left them, Edgar gazing in wonderment at his reflection and Percy salivating over the great feast laid upon the table. 'Water, Percy,' Sir Lancelot requested. 'Lots of hot water.' The knight thrust a large iron-cast pail into the squire's hands.

'Hot water?'

'There is a bathtub,' Sir Lancelot explained, pointing toward the colourful drapes behind him. 'Out the back.'

'A bathtub!' Percy exclaimed. 'Do the pavilion's secrets never end?'

The news was finally enough to break Edgar's infatuation with the mirror. 'Whoever is behind this kindness holds you in high esteem, sir—or they lure you down a path yet revealed.'

Percy spent the last of the day's sunlight heating buckets of water hauled from the riverbank over a fire. As he did so, Edgar departed for the Tipsy Squire. He was to fetch the remainder of Sir Lancelot's possessions from Farley Butterman and, while there, sup an ale or two at the bar. Sir Lancelot begrudgingly admitted that having company after living so long without any was not all bad.

And now, with Percy tending Cedric outside—a squire's chores were many—Sir Lancelot relaxed within his tub of tin and wood. *If there is a better feeling than this, I have yet to experience it.* There are many pleasures in this world, but few are as rewarding as a hot bath after hard graft on a winter's day.

While soaking in his bath, Sir Lancelot pondered the unanswered questions whirling inside his head. Who was his generous benefactor? And more importantly, who was Hellawes' mystery man? Sir Lancelot was no further from unmasking the knight, although he was not short of suspects. Need he look beyond Lord Vortimer? Surely not. Ever had the knave plotted against Arthur and his rule. The witch's prophecy played upon his mind. *Find the brute who bears the scar. You will know him when the time comes. Call it fate or destiny or whatever you want, but this man seeks you out. Pursue this knight to his master, and you shall discover your precious queen.*

Had not Lord Vortimer called him out? And so, too, Sir Roderick? In truth, the young fool was a most unlikely candidate. And what of the scar? *I must hope tomorrow brings answers.* The riddle of the queen's whereabouts needed to be solved quickly. *Each day I linger here is another Guinevere must endure.*

Chapter Thirteen

Morgana's Pets

Sir Kay sagged against Sir Agravain, the knight's upright body a comfort. 'I am all but finished, good sir,' Sir Kay muttered, his voice hoarse, his lips cracked and dry. The knight's tears were long since spent, his clouded eyes red and sore. Fresh blood trickled from an ugly gash across his forehead, dripping from the tip of his broken nose. 'I cannot take anymore.'

Sir Agravain's head snapped sideways. 'Yes, you can,' he urged. 'You must!'

Chained back-to-back, the two men could not see one another. But Sir Agravain had no need to see to know the truth. His friend had given up long ago. The signs of Sir Kay's approaching surrender were plain enough to tell. His head lolled, his spine grew crooked, and he refused to stomach the gaoler's gruel. Piece by piece, his humanity had been taken from him, and with it, his desire to fight.

'You must endure,' Sir Agravain whispered fiercely. He peered through the gloom toward the two black-armoured knights stationed at Morgana's side and shuddered. 'Or else be turned into whatever they are—an abomination against all that is good.'

Sir Agravain wondered which of Camelot's young knights guarded the witch? *It is best not to know.* The very thought was horrifying. *Only Sir Kay and I remain.*

Besides the queen, a dozen men were taken from the green May meadow on that desperate day, and all were beset with injuries inflicted upon the battlefield. Two succumbed to their wounds, three more to torture since, and the rest turned to Morgana's will. Sir Ladinas was the last to be bewitched. *A dreadful pity, the young man had the makings of a fine knight*. Sir Agravain's anger rose like bile. Sir Ladinas had defied Morgana at every turn, but eventually, like the others, his soul became tainted by the witch's evil.

Beside a crackling fire, Morgana and her ill-looking gaoler conversed in whispered tones. 'Sir Kay is ready for breaking, but the other, despite his grey beard and aged bones, not so,' Vexus explained. The man paused to sweep a hunk of lank, black hair from his face, the colour of which was so pale and ghastly that Morgana saw throbbing blue veins beneath the skin.

The creature spends his life shrouded in shadow. His eyes are as black as pitch, his body bent and withered. Morgana could not recall seeing Vexus eat. It was as if the pain drawn from his victims was nourishment enough for his black soul. *The Dark Lord sustains the wretch. Doubtless, a reward for his devotion to the dark arts*. Morgana smiled. She had been rewarded too, many, many times.

'The knight's resilience to my techniques is impressive,' Vexus concluded.

'Then alter your *techniques*,' Morgana scolded. There could be no excuses.

Vexus glanced nervously at Morgana's grim bodyguards. 'Yes, my lady.' He bowed low before slinking into the shadows once more.

How the old man resisted the gaoler's torture, whose methods Morgana knew were meticulously designed to cause maximum discomfort, was perplexing. *Perhaps it would be wise to kill Sir Agravain and be done with it*, she pondered. Yet she was intrigued, and if nothing else, the old knight was a challenge to be resolved.

A man's will cannot be influenced by magic alone. First, it must be broken. The weak-minded are coerced easily enough, their obedience gratefully offered in exchange for the agony to end. And if torture fails to bend their will, what then? Fortuitously, Morgana le Fay's gifts were many, and manipulation of the mind was among her most potent. Lord Mellegrans was evidence of the witch's skills. The man was wrapped around her fingers—a faithful pet at her beck and call.

Stepping from the light of the fire, Morgana moved deeper into the dungeon, disappearing into the dank, fetid dark. She crouched before the beleaguered Sir Kay. The knight's head was slumped forward, his bearded chin resting on his chest, his wild chestnut hair cascading over his swollen face.

Grasping a handful of the knight's knotted curls, Morgana wrenched his head upright so she might gaze into his eyes. 'Brave, Sir Kay,' she began, her voice a soft caress against his tormented skin. 'At last, your suffering is at an end. It is time to concede to me. Pledge your heart and soul into my care. If you do this, you will never know pain again.'

Sir Kay groaned. His half-open, bloodshot eyes stared unblinking into the witch's emerald orbs. He felt drawn into their enchanting depths. They called to his soul—a haunting yet undeniable summoning. Slowly, Sir Kay nodded.

'A wise choice—'

'No!' Sir Agravain cried. He threw back his head, thumping into his comrade's skull, hoping to knock sense into him. 'You must resist the witch's charms, Sir Kay. Do not allow her to poison your heart!'

Morgana released her hold on Sir Kay and leapt to Sir Agravain's side, her anger burning like wildfire. 'Enough!' she howled, striking the troublesome knight a savage blow across the cheek.

With rage threatening to consume her, Morgana withdrew into the shadows lest she cut the wretched knight's throat. 'You have proven to be remarkably resilient, Sir Agravain,' she whispered from the darkness. 'Whilst the others have accepted their destiny, you refuse to submit. It is foolhardy. Your defiance only serves to encourage my efforts.'

Sir Agravain snarled, 'Do your worst, witch. I care not.'

'If you continue to defy me, there will be no end to your anguish, only more torture, day after day. Concede, brave Sir Agravain. Save yourself from this unnecessary torment. Join your comrades and become another of my Dark Knights!'

Lord Mellegrans' arrival into the dismal chamber spared Sir Agravain from further interrogation. At once, Morgana hastened from the shadows to welcome him. She brushed the man's cheek with her ruby lips in greeting. 'You seldom visit here uninvited, my lord. Is all well?'

Morgana's warm touch against Lord Mellegrans' skin was intoxicating, but he forced himself to ignore the woman's persuasive charms. 'Your fascination with my prisoners is a curiosity to me, that is all.'

Morgana smiled innocently. 'I merely check on Vexus' progress,' she answered.

Rejecting Morgana's embrace, Lord Mellegrans stepped instead toward the warmth of the fire. 'Are you sure torturing these men into submission is the best means by which to recruit them?'

Morgana's features twitched with annoyance. 'I share your concerns, sir,' she lied. 'Yet what better way is there to guarantee their loyalty? To fully accept a new master, first the former must be purged from their souls.'

'There is some truth to your words, even if your methods are less than savoury,' Lord Mellegrans said, returning to the stairs. 'I will leave you to your… games.'

Morgana fought to contain her wrath. The man's impertinence was growing. She would need to keep him in check or risk losing him too soon. 'How is our royal guest this morning?' she queried, striving to draw the man's thoughts from the dungeon and its depravities.

Sir Mellegrans halted inside the stairwell. 'As well as anyone who is locked in a tower with no hope of reprieve.'

'Oh, there is always hope, sir, and I suspect that is what fortifies Guinevere's heart.'

'As you say,' Sir Mellegrans replied nonchalantly. 'Your patience to see this precarious scheme to its long, drawn-out conclusion is admirable, but I am afraid my own wears thin.'

Again, anger flared inside Morgana, threatening to destabilise her. Soon, she would not need lecherous oafs such as Lord Mellegrans. Her powers intensified. Her Dark Knights were only the beginning. 'Do not doubt me, *my lord*, nor my *schemes*.'

The woman's tone sent an icy shiver down Lord Mellegrans' spine. 'No, of course not, my lady.'

Morgana swiftly regained her composure. She smiled, sickly and sweet. 'Patience, my lord. The end draws near, I promise.'

*

Staring through the barred window of her tower-top chamber, Guinevere's thoughts wandered. *How many days have passed since my imprisonment?* She had watched the endless forest turn from green to red to brown, and now the trees stood naked like legions of skeletal guards watching her from below. *I have witnessed seasons flourish and fade from this cursed prison, yet none have come for me.* She often imagined her rescuer emerging from the forest, his armour shining like the sun, his gleaming sword sweeping all before him. To her surprise, the gallant knight in question was never her husband. At least, she did not think it was. He was always a nameless knight, his face hidden beneath a silver helmet.

Where is Arthur? Why does he not come? Annoyed by her rising emotions, Guinevere wiped tears from her eyes. *I am not a snivelling girl; I am a queen!* She drew in a long, deep breath of cold winter air as it gusted through the window, and straightening her back, she stiffened her resolve.

When first locked inside the tower, Guinevere had been hell-bent, fighting each day like a wild cat. She screamed and screamed until she could scream no longer. Guinevere attacked the oaken door and the iron bars covering the window day and night. She flew at anyone who dared step foot inside her chamber—servant or soldier, it mattered not. She spat, clawed, kicked, and gouged. Her food was hurled, her water thrown, her bedding and clothing torn and tossed and not once was she told why she was here.

Guinevere's defiance was ignored. In time, she came to realise her behaviour was harming no one but herself—except, of course, for the servants and soldiers she had bruised and scratched during her ill-tempered episodes. Instead, Guinevere chose to play a different game, a patient game—she began to comply. Soon after, her captor was revealed to her, and it had come as no surprise to learn the culprit was none other than Morgana le Fay.

Guinevere had suspected the witch all along. She had forever threatened Arthur's kingdom, an instigator of crooked schemes. The woman's hatred for her brother knew no bounds.

The first meeting between witch and queen was brief. Guinevere had demanded to learn of Morgana's intent and what she had done with her knights. Their terrible screams echoed through the tower from somewhere deep beneath her, haunting her sleepless nights. 'What is it that you hope to gain?'

'What else but coin,' Morgana had said.

'You intend to ransom me?'

'Of course, but alas, Arthur is away fighting his little war, so I fear the negotiations will be painfully ponderous. And as for your knights, you need not worry your pretty head. The cries you hear are not born of anguish but of elation.'

'Elation?'

'Yes, Guinevere, elation. They now serve a new master, and their hearts sing with joy!'

Guinevere was left unconvinced by Morgana's performance. When the witch's visits increased and began involving all manner of peculiar practices, her suspicions grew further. Murmuring in a curious tongue, Morgana would sit cross-legged before her. Sometimes, ethereal lights of green and red swirled and danced in front of Guinevere's eyes, and strange voices, deep and menacing, spoke to her from the shadows.

'What is it that you do?'

'You will see soon enough.'

Guinevere did not understand Morgana's plans, but she was certain of one thing—there would be no ransom.

In the meantime, Guinevere fought to maintain her mind and body. However, the chamber was small, and her rations smaller. Exercising was all but impossible, and the lack of sustenance withered her muscles and sapped her strength. If an opportunity arose, she needed to be able to act, but her ability to do so diminished with each passing day. Instead, Guinevere focussed her efforts and hopes on influencing the minds of her captors. She could not manipulate the witch, but she worked the servants and soldiers who frequented her prison tirelessly. So, too, Lord Mellegrans, who Guinevere ascertained was Morgana's accomplice—her advocate of dark deeds.

Lord Mellegrans was a gullible man, and Guinevere used their meetings to sow the seeds of doubt within his mind. She defined the consequences of his actions and explained in no uncertain terms the true nature of the woman he followed and the terrible master she served. On his last visit, Lord Mellegrans appeared conflicted.

Perhaps he will help me escape after all, Guinevere mused, gazing across the endless forest from her window. The sun had risen. A new day had begun.

Chapter Fourteen

Heroes & Villains

Sir Lancelot pondered the field. The meadow glistened with fallen snow, and fresh flakes of white began swirling from the skies above. *Now, the serious business begins.* The second day of the Great Melee was ever a testing ordeal. *And this day will be more testing than most.* The occasion felt ripe with animosity; an ominous atmosphere cloaked the field. *Today will bear witness to war in all but name.*

Despite Lord Vortimer's loathing for the kings from across the sea and north of the wall, a bargain was struck. Together with King Bagdemagus and the western kings, an alliance was forged to guarantee Sir Gawain's downfall.

The far side of the field bristled with the lances of Arthur's enemies. Sir Lancelot thought Lord Vortimer's host appeared like a winter forest on the march. Their banners lined the horizon, and through the falling snow, Sir Lancelot spotted fanged serpents, white wolves, grey watchtowers, gleaming battleaxes, green eagles, devilish hellhounds, and fiery sunbursts. *And somewhere among them is Hellawes' scarred brute*, he mused. *Yet where?* Discarding Sir Roderick, Lord Vortimer was still his most likely suspect, but the wretch carried no scar that Sir Lancelot knew of. *The day may yet reveal the truth.*

In response to Lord Vortimer's pact, Sir Gawain united Arthur's allies. A gathering of red dragons, black boars, flaming phoenixes, scarlet roses, grey stallions, blue falcons, silver swords, golden grails, and white hammers mobilised to engage the enemy across the meadow.

The time had come to choose sides. Neutrality was not an option, not this day. To stand alone risked being crushed beneath the hammering hooves of two mighty juggernauts.

The marshal's horn blew, clear and true. Soon after, Lord Vortimer's army was pounding through the snow. The crowds of Astolat erupted with excitement, and beneath their feet, the stands groaned and the earth shook with the thundering of warhorses.

'For Arthur!' Sir Gawain roared, leaping into a gallop.

In answer, the combined might of Albion's kings surged over the field. Seldom had the Charge of Seven Kings appeared so magnificent nor felt so daunting to be confined within its ranks. The two forces sped toward one another like earthquakes rumbling from opposite ends of the meadow, and their meeting promised ruin.

For a heartbeat, it seemed as if the whole of Astolat held its breath. And then, with the next, the knights collided together with an almighty crash. For those amongst the crowds who could not bring themselves to watch, the sounds were no less telling—the snorting of warhorses, the stomping of hooves, the roaring of the charge, the clash of lances, the cry of the fallen.

Sir Lancelot punched an emerald eagle from his saddle. Beside him, Sir Lavaine braced a hellhound's lance against his shield. Mercifully, both men emerged from the Charge of Seven Kings unscathed and still in the saddle.

Sir Lancelot reined Cedric in beside his comrade. 'Another lance, sir?' he called to Sir Lavaine.

'Yes, another lance!' Thrill and fear pumped through Sir Lavaine's body. He encouraged his mount to join Sir Lancelot's black steed, and again, the pair cantered into the fray.

Lowering their lances, Sir Lancelot and Sir Lavaine unhorsed their targets, a brace of white wolves. 'Swords!' Sir Lancelot bellowed. In the thick of battle, they found themselves at the beating heart of Lord Vortimer's host. 'Sir Lavaine,' Sir Lancelot yelled. 'We must push through to Sir Gawain and his men.'

The route was obstructed by numerous knights of the fanged serpent. Sir Lancelot slashed and blocked with lightning speed, swiftly forcing progress. Yet behind, Sir Lavaine was beset by a host of men. He fought bravely against so many but eventually was caught by a blow to the head. Disorientated, he was helpless as the enemy's grasping hands hauled him from his saddle. Sir Lavaine was dumped to the churned snow below, where his plight deepened. Lord Vortimer's men stabbed at the fallen knight with their lances, intent on skewering him where he lay.

Sir Lancelot pulled hard on his reins. Cedric reared into the air, the warhorses' flailing hooves knocking the knight's enemies aside. Galloping to Sir Lavaine's aid, Sir Lancelot smashed a black-clad rider from his path before meeting another in battle. The white snake on the man's shield took the brunt of Sir Lancelot's rage, and he was mercilessly battered from his steed. Before arriving at Sir Lavaine's side, the Black Knight's wrath claimed a further three opponents, each unhorsed in quick succession.

Sir Lancelot sheathed his sword and slid sideways in the saddle. Grabbing Sir Lavaine's grasping hand, he hoisted King Pelles' stricken son onto Cedric, but in doing so, a serpent's blade, swift and sharp, struck from the chaos, slashing the knight across the arm.

'Sir Roderick!' Sir Lancelot hissed through clenched teeth. Yet retribution would have to wait. Sir Lancelot burst from the melee and sped to the ropes, depositing the grateful Sir Lavaine into helping hands.

'Caution, sir,' Sir Lavaine advised breathlessly. 'Vortimer's men wield sharp edges and pointed tips!'

Sir Lancelot's injured arm was wet with blood and throbbed more than it should. 'I know, sir. I must warn Sir Gawain of their treachery.' Quickly, he kicked Cedric forward once more. By the time Sir Lancelot rejoined the fighting, he could barely feel his right arm at all. *Sharp edges, pointed tips—and poison*, he mused grimly. He would enjoy despatching Sir Roderick to the dirt. *Yet first, I must seek Sir Gawain.*

En route, Sir Lancelot strapped his shield to his wounded arm. Then, pounding toward the mass of entangled men and mounts, he snatched up a discarded lance sticking from the earth. Wielding the weapon with his left hand, he crunched into the hard-pressed horde of bodies with terrifying speed. A quartet of blue-faced Northmen fell foul to Sir Lancelot's charge—the Black Knight's lance toppling them one after the other. Replacing the lance with his sword, he battered eagles, wolves, and hellhounds from his path.

The Pendragon drew near, billowing in the gathering winds above the battlefield. The snow thickened—a frozen deluge to obstruct the eyes and confuse the senses.

Through the swirling white skies, Sir Lancelot spied Lord Vortimer's fanged serpent. The black and white standard had reached the dragon. Sir Lancelot surged onward. He stopped a lance against his shield before sweeping a snake from the saddle. Pushing on, Sir Lancelot glimpsed Sir Gawain through the mass of writhing bodies. The knight of the Round Table shone amidst the snow, his scale armour gleaming as if he were a Roman general of old.

'Beware the fanged serpent, Sir Gawain,' Sir Lancelot called. 'The snake's bite is deadly and dripping with venom!'

Sir Gawain acknowledged Sir Lancelot with a brisk nod before the enemy swarmed him. Lord Vortimer spearheaded the assault against the Round Table knight, encouraged by his advantage. Even so, blunted blade or not, Sir Gawain was more than a match for the outcast prince. Their swords clashed with a metallic clang, resounding far and wide.

Sir Lancelot protected Sir Gawain's blindside, unhorsing opposing knights seeking to out-manoeuvre the champion—and all with his left hand. His right arm was numb below the elbow, but now was not the time to concern himself with the injury.

For a fleeting moment, Sir Lancelot spied Sir Tarquin through the snow. The giant led a posse of Tower Knights against Sir Gawain's flank, but Sir Galleron, riding at the forefront of a strong contingent of Lyonesse knights, intercepted and forced him back.

A score of riders burst between Sir Lancelot and Sir Gawain. Outnumbered, the two champions of Camelot, past and present, defended furiously, using sword and shield to hold the many-pronged raid at bay.

The crowds of Astolat cheered as their favourite knights survived one attack after another. Yet Lord Vortimer's brazen host threatened to overrun them.

Rallying behind King Borticus and Sir Galleron, Sir Gawain's allies kicked their warhorses back into the melee. Lord Vortimer sensed the tide was turning against him. Mustering a final effort, he and his best men launched themselves at Sir Gawain.

The crowds shrieked in dismay. How could Sir Gawain prevail against so many? The folk of Astolat despaired at the thought of the tournament progressing without him. Yet, it was another of the crowd's favourites who was at hand to save the champion from Lord Vortimer's clutches. Not King Borticus the Boar, nor Sir Galleron the Lion, but Sir Galaad le Noir, the Black Knight.

With Lady Elayne's red ribbon streaming from his helmet, he drove Lord Vortimer from his saddle and into the snow. The stands erupted with joy, 'The Black Knight! The Black Knight!'

Soon after Lord Vortimer was sent sprawling, the master of the games drew the contest to an end with another shrill blast of his shining horn.

'You fight well, Sir Galaad,' Sir Gawain praised as the knights made their way from the field.

Behind them, Lord Vortimer was pulled from the snow by his lackeys. Once hauled to his feet, he shoved their helping hands aside, seething with anger as he watched Sir Gawain and his saviour, the so-called *Black Knight*, leave the meadow to deafening acclaim. His dark eyes narrowed. *They will pay for this insult*, he promised.

Edgar and Percy were at hand to escort Sir Lancelot through the masses. Edgar was hard-fought to keep the excitable hordes at arm's length, and once again, he was compelled to employ his staff of twisted birch to clear safe passage. Many a limb or rump was left stinging and red raw as a consequence.

Once returned to Champion's Meadow, the Black Knight's adoring support dispersed. The ride across the field to the pavilion was a snowy blur. Sir Lancelot sagged low in the saddle, his poisoned wound worsening. Sliding from Cedric's back, he required Edgar's hand to steady him. 'Are you well, sir?' the veteran asked.

Sir Lancelot tore the helmet from his head and tossed it into the snow. 'I am poisoned, Edgar,' he replied feebly. The knight's black curls dripped with perspiration, and his bearded face was deathly pale. He twitched his head toward the useless right arm hanging limp at his side. 'Sir Roderick's blade,' he mumbled incoherently. 'It is but a scratch.'

'Scratch or otherwise, the scoundrel has found his mark, Sir Galaad.' Between them, Edgar and Percy helped Sir Lancelot inside the pavilion. 'To bed, good sir knight.'

'Nonsense,' Sir Lancelot slurred, swaying one way and then another. 'I have been poisoned before.'

'That may be, sir, but in my experience, being poisoned previously does not mean you cannot be again. And by the look of you, I'd say you've been poisoned good.'

Edgar and Percy dumped Sir Lancelot atop his bed, where the feverish knight attempted a half-hearted bid to rise again before promptly forsaking the effort.

'Percy, go at once to the castle,' Edgar instructed. 'Fetch Lady Elayne and do not return without her.'

As Percy disappeared outside, Edgar set about boiling a pan of water to tend to Sir Lancelot's wound. Removing the knight's armour, he stripped the blood-soaked leather from his body. Sir Lancelot was right. The injury was nothing more than a shallow cut to the upper arm, but the wound was angry and oozing foul bile, the flesh below the gash red and inflamed.

Edgar treated the wound with a clean rag, rinsing the worst of the odious discharge with the boiled water. Sir Lancelot had drifted into a fitful sleep when Sir Lavaine appeared.

'Do you bring your sister, sir?' Edgar asked.

'My sister? No, I come to offer Sir Galaad my gratitude and carry an invite to dine with Lord Astolat at the castle this evening.'

'Alas, my lord, Sir Galaad is gravely ill—poisoned by Sir Roderick's blade. I sent Sir Galaad's squire to fetch Lady Elayne from the castle and hoped she was with you.'

Sir Lavaine was shocked. 'No, sir, I have not encountered your squire. Perchance, he evaded me en route.' He thought for a moment. 'To be certain, sir, I will return to the castle.' Sir Lavaine hurried from the pavilion. 'I will make all haste!' he called, vanishing into the darkening, snow-laden skies.

Night had fallen before Percy returned. 'Where have you been?' Edgar demanded. 'Sir Galaad tosses and turns in his bed with a fever.'

'Fear not,' Percy said, 'Lady Elayne approaches, see?' He held open the pavilion to reveal a distant lantern dancing closer across the meadow. Percy dashed back into the falling snow to assist the princess from her mount.

Cloaked in fur, Lady Elayne bustled inside, her beautiful face a picture of concern beneath her cowl. 'Out!' she said, ordering both Edgar and Percy from the pavilion before rushing to Sir Lancelot atop his bed. 'Lord, have mercy! Not again.' She rested a hand upon the knight's burning brow. Sir Lancelot twitched and murmured at her touch. 'Sir Galaad, can you hear me?' She glanced anxiously at his injured arm. Edgar had wrapped the affected area, but she saw how the bandage was wet through. The wound yet wept. 'It is I, Elayne,' she whispered softly.

'Elayne?' Sir Lancelot's eyes crept open. 'What have you done with Edgar?'

Lady Elayne scowled. 'The man wraps your arm when all know an infected wound requires fresh air.' She shook her head. 'You are scarcely free from the wyrm's awful poison, and now I fear this second dose will succeed where the first failed.'

Sir Lancelot took her hand in his. 'Do not fret, good lady. I will prevail as I did before.'

Lady Elayne smiled, but her blue eyes remained full of worry. She lifted his limp hand to her ruby lips, brushing them against his burning skin. 'My father and I thank you for your gallantry. My brother means much to me, as do you.' She lowered her eyes. 'I do not know what I would do if I lost either.'

Gently, Sir Lancelot squeezed her hand. 'I had my suspicions the pavilion was your doing. It has a woman's touch.'

'If I had told you I was responsible, you would have denied me. My father and I thought it a good idea. We both knew you would refuse Lord Astolat's invitation to lodge at the castle, so I needed an alternative, somewhere easily spotted so I might find you during the night.' Lady Elayne's eyes caught Sir Lancelot's with a mischievous glint. 'And in any case, you deserve such luxury. Not only for your heroics in Corbyn but for your loyalty at this tourney. And, not least, for preserving my brother's life today.'

'It seems you know me all too well, my lady,' Sir Lancelot answered weakly, and with each whispered word, his voice faded until, eventually, he spoke no more.

Chapter Fifteen

A Mother's Love

Sir Lancelot's dreams were of snakes and blue-faced demons. A terrible fever held him within its tightening grasp, slowly choking the life from his soul. He awoke with a start, his bedsheets slick with sweat, his skin burning, his bones aching, his wound throbbing. Lady Elayne slept beside him, her head cradled in her arms at his bedside.

She is fairer asleep than she is awake. If that was possible. *What have I done?* The poor girl was infatuated with him, and he had done little to dissuade her even though he loved another. *She deserves better.* For a fleeting moment, he felt the fight leave him. Would it not be easier to yield? Yet, who would save Guinevere? Who would keep the demons at bay? Lord Vortimer's sneering face swirled inside his delirious mind, and then Sir Roderick's, too. They mocked his weakness, grinning and laughing. Yet somewhere in a distant corner of his thoughts was birdsong—a familiar melody, beautiful and enchanting, growing stronger and stronger. The sneering faces fled, chased from his fever dreams by a sky turned dark with countless blackbirds.

'Drink.'

Through bleary eyes, Sir Lancelot saw a woman's face leaning over him, and it was not Lady Elayne's. 'Mother?'

Gently, Nimue lifted her son's head. 'Drink,' she repeated, pressing a cup to his parched lips.

The liquid was cool but bitter on his tongue. Sir Lancelot coughed and spluttered feebly. 'Why have you come?'

Abruptly, Nimue dropped Sir Lancelot's head back against his pillows. 'Why have I come?' She narrowed her eyes and scowled like only a mother could. 'To save you from her, of course.' Nimue jerked her head sideways toward the sleeping beauty beside him.

'She means well.'

Nimue's face softened. 'She does, and in fairness, she was right to leave the wound to breathe. Although I am not entirely sure what the girl has smeared upon the gash?' Nimue dabbed a finger into the ointment before touching it to her lips. 'Ah, nothing more than honey, nettle, and rose. Her concoction smells and tastes well enough, but it will do little to remedy the condition.' She winked. 'Fear not. Your mother's medicine may smell and taste foul, but when has it ever failed you?'

Sir Lancelot was already beginning to feel the effects. A wondrous sense of relief washed through him, numbing his aches and pains and cooling his searing flesh and bones. 'Thank you,' he whispered.

'You will be weak on the morrow, but the substance has been driven from your body. In future, you really must refrain from getting yourself poisoned. At least you will now be immune to this particular brand of devilry, but not others, so please be careful.'

Sir Lancelot smiled warmly. 'I will do my best, I promise.'

'Well, having watched you survive your encounter with the Saxon witch, Hellawes, I could not see you fall prey to something as simple as a poisoned sword.' Nimue studied her son, her face becoming stern once again. 'You know what you must do, so why do you hesitate? What are you afraid of?'

Sir Lancelot chose not to answer. *Find the brute who bears the scar. You will know him when the time comes. Call it fate or destiny or whatever you want, but this man seeks you out.*

'Even parading as the Black Knight, you accrue fame, unwanted or not. It is in your blood. You are a born leader of men, inspiring them to good deeds and greatness. You are the son of King Ban from across the Narrow Sea, a king without a kingdom. When your father fell fighting for Uther, I raised you, knowing that destiny would someday summon you to do her bidding. That day has come. It is time you returned to the world, my son. Arthur needs you. Albion needs you. Guinevere needs you.'

Sir Lancelot nodded. 'Soon, Mother,' he whispered. 'Soon, Sir Lancelot will return.'

Nimue stood to leave, but before she did so, her eyes lingered on the sleeping princess. 'The girl is with child,' she declared. 'She does not realise yet, but I thought it best you know.'

Despite his malaise, Sir Lancelot sat bolt upright in his bed. 'With child? My child?'

'Yes, Son. With your child.'

'But… how?'

Nimue raised an eyebrow.

'The night at the Tipsy Squire? How can you tell so soon?'

'Am I not a witch?' she replied, amused. 'She glows as all expectant mothers do.'

*

The following day, Sir Lancelot awoke refreshed and free of Sir Roderick's poison. He turned his head to find Lady Elayne sleeping soundly. For a time, he watched her as she dreamed.

Truly, she is fairer than a May morning. And now, knowing she bore his child inside her, she seemed fairer still. But swiftly, a darkness swept through him. *And yet, I rush to Guinevere*. A war raged inside his soul, an inner conflict threatening to tear him apart from within. The honourable action was to do right by Lady Elayne. Yet, he would not—could not—forsake Guinevere. Albion's queen was in terrible peril, and his duty was clear no matter his feelings toward her. As a knight of the Round Table, he was charged with doing everything in his power to rescue Guinevere and end Morgana's treachery.

Slipping from the covers, Sir Lancelot dressed for battle. The Great Melee was over. Now, the joust would begin.

If I have not unmasked my foe before the day is done, I shall have no choice but to unmask myself. His mother's words lingered inside Sir Lancelot's mind: *What are you afraid of?* Sir Lancelot knew the answer. *I am afraid of myself*. But he could not run from who he was forever. The time had come to step from the shadows and reclaim his rightful place by Arthur's side.

Emerging from the pavilion, Sir Lancelot was met by a flabbergasted Edgar. The old soldier had kept watch through the cold night while Percy slept beneath the awning with Cedric for company. 'How are you recovered?' he exclaimed. 'By Bran's beard, but we thought you wouldn't make it through the night!'

Sir Lancelot gazed out across the meadow. Lighting the eastern horizon, the sun's golden rays began to shine. The winter storm had passed, and now the skies were clear. The land lay smothered beneath an all-encompassing blanket of white. Muffled by the snow, the sounds of dawn were subdued—the cawing of crows, the shrill cry of a distant vixen, the rushing of the river, the din of a camp coming to life.

Sir Lancelot faced Edgar and winked. 'As I said, I have been poisoned before.'

Edgar snorted like a horse, a plume of warm breath lifting into the frosty air from beneath the man's padded hood. 'I'll wager Lady Elayne is the only cause of your recovery, sir. It seems the princess is more than just a pretty face.'

'Indeed.' His mood pensive, Sir Lancelot returned his gaze across the meadow. The camp was stirring. Squires and attendants roused their masters from their slumber. A full day's jousting lay ahead. Come nightfall, the tournament's contenders would number less than two and twenty.

'I have news that I think will please you, Sir Galaad,' Edgar announced, and he spoke in such a way that Sir Lancelot was at once intrigued by his friend's words. 'After sundown, while you tossed abed fighting your poison, there came a messenger bearing the draw for the joust.' Edgar grinned. 'By chance, you face Sir Roderick.'

Now, it was Sir Lancelot's turn to snort. 'A welcome twist of fate, Edgar, or mayhap those who decide such things thought the match would draw the crowds? Either way, Sir Roderick will fall, poisoned lance or not.'

A rustling beside Cedric caused the horse to whinny. Percy's head protruded from a great bundle of furs.

Edgar booted snow into the young man's face. 'Come, Sir Squire. Your duties await. Your master must make ready for the joust!'

'Joust?' Percy mumbled, eyes half-closed and brain addled. 'We must make ready his grave, mores the like.' It was then he noticed Sir Lancelot stood above him, and he was very much alive. 'Truly, a miracle, sir!' Percy blurted, scrambling to his feet. 'You are made from fine stock and strong bones to have seen off such a fearful curse!'

Sir Lancelot shook his head at the floundering youth before re-entering the pavilion. As he moved across to the bed, Lady Elayne was waking. Sir Lancelot sat beside her and watched as she opened her blue eyes.

Immediately, Lady Elayne's face lightened. 'Praise be! You live!' Lunging forward, she wrapped her arms around the knight's neck and buried her head into his long hair. 'I thought I was going to lose you this time.' Tears of happiness welled in her eyes.

'So everyone keeps telling me,' Sir Lancelot whispered. 'Yet how can a man surrender to death when he is so loved?' For a moment, Sir Lancelot became serious. He held Lady Elayne at arm's length. 'My lady, I must ask a boon of you and your father.'

The request was met with a curious frown. 'Of course,' Lady Elayne said. 'Come to the castle tonight. I will arrange an audience with my father.' She tilted her head and narrowed her blue eyes. 'And what do you require of me, pray tell?'

'Be at the meeting tonight, and you shall see.'

Lady Elayne pursed her lips. 'So be it. Sir Galaad le Noir will keep his secrets for one more day.' She gripped Sir Lancelot's hands tightly. 'Be careful out there today. You have made enemies.'

*

Sir Erkenthorn of Logres was punched from his steed. The sight of his limp body launching skyward before crunching deep into the snow had the audience bellowing his victor's name, 'Sir Gawain! Sir Gawain!' The knight of the Round Table's lance had flicked up at the last instant, catching Sir Erkenthorn cold and slamming him from the saddle.

The action came thick and fast. As soon as Sir Gawain was cheered from the field and the battered Sir Erkenthorn helped away on unsteady legs, another pair of combatants manoeuvred into position. The giant Sir Tarquin waited to charge, his mighty midnight stallion pawing the trampled snow beneath its hooves with excitement.

At the other end, Sir Castleton, a young knight of Dumnonia, struggled to control his skittish grey mare. The beast reared and danced, spooked by the baying crowds eager for the contest to begin.

Suddenly, they were away, and the knights were pounding at each other at terrifying speeds. Sir Tarquin was an imposing sight. He bore down on Sir Castleton like a huge black bear hunting a helpless stag. Yet the stag was swift and lithe, and Sir Tarquin's incoming lance was skillfully evaded while Sir Castleton caught the giant a heavy blow to the torso.

Somehow, the two knights held firm and were each replenished with fresh lances. Wheeling their mounts, they faced one another for a second tilt. Sir Castleton kicked his grey mare onward. Sir Tarquin lurched forward. At the centre of the course, the mismatched men collided. Again, the young Dumnonian drove his lance into his rival's body, but such was Sir Tarquin's strength he rode the challenge before crashing his lance into the antlered stag upon Sir Castleton's shield. Sir Castleton was unable to absorb the blow as Sir Tarquin had, and he cartwheeled from his mount into the snow.

The crowds booed and jeered Sir Tarquin. Sir Castleton had become a favourite in the stands, especially among the ladies and maidens who had grown fond of the knight's golden locks and baby-faced charm.

Next, another crowd favourite took to the field, the chivalrous and mysterious Black Knight, cheered and cherished by all Astolat. While not as burly or imposing as the giant Sir Tarquin, Sir Galaad le Noir was equally as menacing. Encased in black, save for Lady Elayne's scarlet favour, he looked a daunting prospect.

As the marshal of the games introduced Sir Galaad, the watching audience erupted with support, and like the detested Sir Tarquin before him, the Black Knight's opponent was heartlessly heckled. The knight was garbed in Lord Vortimer's colours of black and white. Emblazoned upon his shield was the white-fanged viper, and crested atop his helmet a spitting snake. Rumour was rife. Sir Roderick was accused of trying to poison the Black Knight, and all had witnessed his dastardly attempts to maim Sir Lavaine after he had fallen during the melee.

The marshal's trumpet electrified the spectators into a frenzy. It seemed as if the whole of Astolat had emptied to cheer the Black Knight to victory. For a moment, Sir Roderick appeared ready to concede the joust, but the presence of his master peering from the stands was enough to spur him into action.

Sir Roderick tore his gaze from Lord Vortimer and concentrated on his challenger. The Black Knight was fast approaching. Inside his helmet, the young knight's breath came in ragged gasps. Sweat stung his eyes and blurred his vision. He kicked on, fear gripping his heart and cramping his muscles. He lowered his lance with a trembling hand…

There followed a jolting crash. The wind was knocked from Sir Roderick's body. For a time, he could see nothing except clear blue sky. And then he was thumping into the snow, and all he could hear were the chanting crowds of Astolat, 'The Black Knight! The Black Knight!'

Chapter Sixteen

Sir Lancelot du Lac

The night was clear, and the stars shone high above Astolat's beamed dwellings and timber halls. Cloaked in black, Sir Lancelot rode Cedric through the town, passing dark sleeping households as he travelled the streets, winding ever upwards. Earlier, the same dirt-packed paths and cobbled thoroughfares echoed with frivolity but now were as silent as a tomb.

Perched on the high ground above the river, Castle Astolat gleamed in the moonlight. Although not as grand as Camelot nor so dramatic as Tintagel, the castle was still a commanding fortress with high white walls and towering spires pointing toward the sky.

The short journey allowed Sir Lancelot a chance to reflect. The day had passed in a blur of thundering hooves and clashing lances, and by dusk, Hellawes' mystery knight remained frustratingly elusive. Time was running short. Lord Astolat would hail a new champion on the morrow, and with the tournament ended, Sir Lancelot's hopes of finding Guinevere would be all but over.

Sir Lancelot dismounted at the foot of the north tower. A small sally port set in the white stone opened, and from within the secret entrance, a hooded figure holding a flickering lantern beckoned him inside. Leading Cedric by the reins, the knight entered the castle.

Securing the door, the figure drew back their cowl. 'You can leave Cedric here,' Lady Elayne instructed. 'Come, they are waiting for you.'

Lady Elayne led Sir Lancelot up a twisting stairwell. Ascending until they gained the uppermost level, the pair emerged into a circular chamber where Sir Lancelot was greeted by Lady Elayne's father, King Pelles of Corbyn, and a second man.

'Sir Gawain!' Sir Lancelot exclaimed happily, gripping the warrior by the hand.

'Greetings, friend,' Sir Gawain replied. Yet it was plain to see by the champion's baffled expression that he neither knew the identity of the hooded stranger before him nor the reason for this clandestine meeting.

'Having guessed the purpose for this gathering, at least in part, I presumed to invite Arthur's champion,' King Pelles explained to Sir Lancelot. 'I thought it wise Sir Gawain was present to witness your announcement—or should I say unveiling? I hope I have guessed right and have not overstepped my authority?'

Sir Lancelot nodded. 'You guess well, my king, and as always, your wisdom is sound and well met.'

The Black Knight drew the hood from his head.

At first, Sir Gawain was none the wiser, but then realisation flowered across the knight's face like sunlight piercing storm clouds. 'Is it really you?'

Sir Lancelot grinned. 'Yes, my old friend.'

The two warriors embraced warmly. Sir Gawain could not pull his gaze from Sir Lancelot's face. 'It appears you are now more beard than man.' He gripped his friend by the shoulders. 'By the old gods and the new, it is good to see you again. Where have you been? What happened?'

Sir Lancelot's smile faded. 'It is a long story for another time,' he said quietly. 'Yet now that I am returned, I request your help, and yours also, good king, in a matter of foremost importance.'

'What is it that you ask of us, Sir Lancelot?' King Pelles queried.

Sir Lancelot felt strange hearing his name spoken freely after all this time. He glanced toward Lady Elayne to gauge her reaction—of which there was none. 'You do not appear surprised, my lady?' He raised a questioning eyebrow at King Pelles.

King Pelles held his hands up in protest. 'I promise you. I have said nothing.'

Lady Elayne smiled. 'I am no fool, sir,' she declared. 'Did you really think I did not know? After caring for you for so long, how could I not? Delirium loosens the tongue, and fever-dreams reveal the truth.'

'Why did you not say, my lady?'

'A man's secrets are his own. And besides, a woman in command of a man's secrets is mindful of his intentions without him worrying about what she thinks.'

I pray she does not know all my secrets, Sir Lancelot thought. His soul was burdened by shame, and news of Lady Elayne's condition only added to the load. *What a tangled web I weave.* For now, he pushed his guilt aside. 'On the morrow, Sir Galaad le Noir will be no more. Nonetheless, for my transformation to achieve the desired effect, I must look the part.' He had no need to elaborate further, not when his wild appearance spoke volumes.

'And I assume this is where I come into play?' Lady Elayne said, eyeing Sir Lancelot with amusement. 'It seems I have much work to do. I must be both tailor and barber.'

It was a demeaning task for a princess, but until the announcement, the fewer people knowing the truth, the better.

'Thank you, Elayne,' Sir Lancelot said. 'I am forever in your debt.' *In more ways than you will ever know.*

King Pelles stroked his beard thoughtfully. 'Leave the details to me. Lord Astolat and I will ensure your return will be well received.'

King Pelles beckoned his guests into chairs beside the chamber's fire. The flames crackled and danced in the hearth, the warmth a welcome friend when the night was cold and full of enemies. 'I am pleased that you have decided to return,' continued the king. 'But tell me, why now? Why here?'

'Because I must. And know that I do not do so lightly.' Sir Lancelot settled himself into a chair and stared into the jumping flames. 'The reasons for my exile are mine alone to know, but now it seems I must step into the light once again if I am to find my queen.'

'What knowledge do you command of the queen?' Sir Gawain demanded, surging to his feet.

'There is a knight here at the tourney linked to Guinevere's disappearance, and only Sir Lancelot du Lac's return will draw him from the shadows.'

Lady Elayne scowled. 'You use yourself as bait?' She shook her head. 'Flirting with death as often as you do makes me question your commitment to living.'

Sir Lancelot met Lady Elayne's accusing blue eyes. 'I am committed to what must be done, my lady.'

'How have you come by this information?' King Pelles asked, pawing at his beard once more.

'The Saxon princess, Hellawes.'

'Hellawes? You cannot trust a witch!' Sir Gawain blustered scornfully.

'Witch or not, she speaks the truth,' Sir Lancelot answered. 'Hellawes' knight will deliver us to Morgana and, in turn, to Guinevere.'

'You believe Morgana le Fay has the queen?' King Pelles said, surprised by the accusation. 'She would not dare.'

'Morgana's powers increase, and with them her ambition. The witch's magic cloaks her whereabouts. It is the reason neither hide nor hair of our queen can be found.'

'I think you are mistaken, Sir Lancelot,' the king argued. 'You pursue a culprit when there is none. At least, not human. If the queen was abducted by Morgana or some other villain, why was a ransom not issued? I fear as we all do that Guinevere was snatched by demons for a purpose I do not know nor wish to contemplate.'

'King Pelles is right,' Sir Gawain said gravely. 'In your stead, Arthur charged me with Guinevere's return. I have scoured the lands from the western wilds to the northern mountains, and there has been no word nor sign.' The knight shook his head lamentably. 'I must admit, it is hard to take. I have little desire to return to my king without news or hope. In truth, I am here at Astolat in desperate search of hearsay and rumour—a crumb of evidence to galvanise my efforts.'

'I have more than crumbs, my friend. You need only trust me.'

Sir Gawain studied his dishevelled comrade, and after a time, he nodded. 'So be it. Tell me what I must do.'

*

Sir Lancelot withdrew to his pavilion deep in the night. He found Edgar asleep underneath a heap of furs beside the dying embers of the fire, but Percy was nowhere to be seen. Doubtless, the youth had passed out after drinking late at the Blushing Maiden or the Tipsy Squire. Sir Lancelot did not blame the boy. It was an exciting time to be living in Astolat. Each and every inn was full to bursting with bawdy bards, drunken drinkers, and merry minstrels. Sir Lancelot wondered which lucky hostelry had the pleasure of Gaston le Grece's inebriated company. The Minstrels of Knoberton enjoyed nothing better than performing to an audience. *That said,* Sir Lancelot thought, *it is debatable whether any performing occurred.* He smiled. It was hard not to like the motley crew. *Gaston and his friends will have a new tale to tell on the morrow.* Sir Lancelot felt uneasy at the prospect. How would Astolat's crowds react to his unmasking? And would Sir Lancelot's return provoke Hellawes' mystery knight into action? One thing was for certain: this would be his last night spent in Lady Elayne's pavilion. The Black Knight had enemies, but Sir Lancelot had more. *It is a pity,* he thought. *I have grown fond of my tent and its comforts.*

Before taking to his bed, Sir Lancelot retrieved Secace from the weapon's hiding place. He had slid the sword between the animal skins stitched into the pavilion's canvas lining.

Sir Lancelot sprawled amongst the furs upon his bed with Secace beside him, questioning Lord Vortimer's resolve for ordering his throat slit in the dark. *Vortimer and men like him are craven. He will plot revenge, but it will come to nothing. He does not have the stomach for vengeance.* But it paid to be prepared for the worst.

The night was full of twisted nightmares. More than once, Sir Lancelot awoke with a start. He dreamt of cloaked assassins and red-eyed demons, even drawing the Sword of Shining when he believed himself under attack. The flashing blade summoned Edgar, who, brandishing his own sword, dashed into the pavilion expecting trouble.

The morning finally arrived, crisp and cold once again. Rising early, Sir Lancelot redeposited Secace amidst the animal skins above his bed before making his way into town to meet the blacksmith. The last day of the tournament was here, and it was time for single combat. Blunted swords were the weapon of choice, and as such, Sir Lancelot wanted to choose a blade suited to his needs, something with the right balance and feel.

Having secured an adequate sword from Bergan, Sir Lancelot was surprised to find a visitor awaiting his return inside the pavilion. 'Lord Astolat,' he said in greeting. 'It is an honour, my lord.'

Lord Astolat shook his shaggy white mane. 'No, Sir Lancelot, the honour is mine,' The old man replied, bowing low. 'Your name has become legend, sir. And now two legends are made whole—Sir Lancelot and the Black Knight, the one and same. By Bran's beard, your revelation will send Astolat into a frenzy!'

'You flatter me, lord,' Sir Lancelot replied uncomfortably. As ever, praise rested awkwardly upon his broad shoulders.

'Piffle! You, good sir, are a living legend. Other than Arthur himself—who let us be honest, lacks your flair for the dramatic—there is no one to match your fame and standing, not even the illustrious Sir Gawain.'

Sir Lancelot smiled courteously, but all the while, he was cringing inside. Lord Astolat was a showman, and Sir Lancelot began feeling like the man's prized bullock waiting to be paraded before the salivating masses.

'Not in all my days have I felt so invigorated!' Lord Astolat's bushy white eyebrows and long bristling moustaches twitched upon his wrinkled face as he quivered with delight. 'King Pelles was at my door in the early hours before dawn. Yet, never have I been so pleased to be roused from my slumber with such tidings. Rest assured, the preparations are made. Your return will be announced by bards and trumpets. The crowds will rejoice at the sight of Albion's lost champion like never before!'

Sir Lancelot's heart sank. His solitary existence was set to be shattered into a thousand pieces. *I will become a freak, poked and prodded like a caged animal.* Nonetheless, if his exuberant comeback granted results, all was well and good.

'I have something for you,' Lord Astolat continued. 'A knight of legend you shall be!' He shuffled aside to reveal a suit of gleaming armour laid out atop the furs on Sir Lancelot's bed. 'It was my father's,' he explained. 'He, too, was a great champion in his day. Alas, I was not made for battle.'

The armour was a wonderful piece—a majestic coat of layered silver scales accompanied by greaves, guards, gauntlets, and a beautifully worked red-plumed helmet resting on a fine black cape.

'Black, silver, and red,' Lord Astolat declared. 'The colours of your past entwined to symbolise your future.'

Chapter Seventeen

Vengeance

Sir Tarquin blocked with his shield before counterattacking with a series of savage strokes. Like a blacksmith's hammer, the giant's blade pounded against the red rose emblazoned upon Sir Galleron's shield. The Lyonesse knight defended staunchly, but Sir Tarquin was relentless, each swing of his sword like being rammed by an antlered stag.

Sir Galleron struggled to keep the giant at arm's length. Then he stumbled. Pain erupted inside his body. His defences were breached.

Sensing victory, Sir Tarquin advanced, crashing his blade against the rose of Lyonesse over and over.

'I yield!' Sir Galleron cried, finally beaten into submission.

Sir Tarquin chose not to listen and continued battering the beleaguered knight even after he was forced to the snowy ground.

'I yield, sir!'

The crowds of Astolat booed the unchivalrous Sir Tarquin. However, their interest became distracted. Waiting to enter the arena was a knight in shining armour, a knight of splendour, a knight they did not recognise. Encased within a magnificent coat of gleaming scales, the man sat astride his mighty warhorse as if he were Bran the Blessed returned from the Otherworld to vanquish all before him and claim Astolat's prize.

A hush descended. Sir Galleron trudged from the field unnoticed, but Sir Tarquin remained watching with intrigue.

Suddenly, the quiet was broken by a fanfare of blaring trumpets, and when the shrill notes faded, a band of minstrels burst into song. They performed a stirring sequence on pipes and strings, and hollering above the captivating tune was a portly, ruddy-cheeked bard whose booming voice carried to the back of the stands and beyond. He was draped in a colourful cloak of swirls and wore bright red breeches that appeared big enough to accommodate an extra pair of legs.

'We all adore heroes of myth and legend,' Gaston le Grece bellowed. 'Tristan, Caradoc, Boudica, to name but few!'

The spectators inside the crowded arena murmured in agreement. To house Astolat's hordes on the tourney's final day, a second stand had been hastily erected opposite the first and a third to the south. The north side remained open for the comings and goings of the competitors, including an area for those onlookers lacking the coin to watch from the stands. Not an inch of meadow, tree branch or rooftop was unoccupied.

'Yet it is rare indeed to have the opportunity, nay, privilege to encounter a true hero in the flesh.'

The people of Astolat turned to one another with animated expressions and rutted brows. Who was this knight in silver?

'Respectable folk of Albion,' Gaston began, allowing the tension to build. 'It is with great pleasure that I present to you the Slayer of the Wolf of Arden, Killer of the Creature of Crumbracken, Destroyer of the Wicked Wyrm of Corbyn, and Defiler of the Giant Goat of Gorsten Gorge!'

The spectators cheered louder and louder with each announcement.

'Fair folk of Astolat bear witness as the mysterious Black Knight is revealed. Bow your heads in reverence for the return of Albion's lost son. Behold, the champion of champions, Sir Lancelot du Lac!'

As the crowds stared in astonishment, the knight pulled his red-plumed helmet from his head. Then, reaching down, he claimed his shield from the silver-haired squire at his side. The shield was black save for a roaring red dragon emblazoned at its centre.

'Pendragon!' the crowds gasped.

The knight's face was clean-shaven, and his dark hair was shorn. Gone were the Black Knight's unruly beard and knotted locks.

The folk of Astolat exploded in celebration. They jumped up and down, hugging and kissing one another in an outpouring of joy. 'Sir Lancelot has returned!' they cried. 'Arthur's champion lives!' Maidens swooned, lords and ladies gaped like trout, boys and girls squealed with unbridled delight... but Sir Tarquin roared with rage.

Snorting like a bull, the brute charged. He knew he ought to wait and bide his time, but the raw emotion boiling inside the knight's body could not be contained. Here was the man Sir Tarquin had scoured the country to find. Here was the man responsible for his brother's demise. *I will slay him here and now in front of his adoring fans. His blood will stain the snow scarlet, and at long last, my brother's soul will be avenged.*

The giant knight lowered his bull-helmeted head. Then, summoning his immense strength, he charged Sir Lancelot's mighty stallion, shouldering man and beast into the snow.

Lady Elayne stared aghast from the stands. Her father, King Pelles, clasped her hands reassuringly. 'Do not fret, Daughter,' he said. 'Sir Lancelot knows what he is doing.'

'What *is* he doing?' Sir Lavaine questioned, sourly tempted to intervene on his friend's behalf.

Sir Lancelot was due to fight King Borticus, the Boar of Badon. Yet now, determined to stop Sir Tarquin's madness, King Borticus drew his blade and entered the arena.

Sir Lancelot waved King Borticus back. 'Fear not,' he said, gathering himself after his fall. 'If this knight has grievances with me, then so be it.' Sir Lancelot secured his helmet, strapped his shield tight, and drew his sword.

'Are you certain, Sir Lancelot?' King Borticus called. 'The brigand must answer for his conduct.'

'I am certain,' Sir Lancelot replied. 'And mark my words; he will answer for his actions.'

The folk of Astolat could not believe what they were witnessing. Not a game but a duel. And by the murderous displayed by Sir Lancelot's accuser, a duel to the death. The stands burst with support for their returning champion, singing his name until their throats were dry and their voices hoarse, 'Sir Lancelot! Sir Lancelot!'

So, at last, here is Hellawes' brute. Now, the game begins. Sir Lancelot had not expected such a swift response to his unmasking. In truth, he could not have hoped for a more fortuitous outcome. Sir Tarquin's unlawful conduct, witnessed by all Astolat, would mean banishment. *And who else will he run to but his mistress, Morgana le Fay.*

'I will have my vengeance!' Sir Tarquin bellowed, chasing his silver-clad nemesis across the arena.

Sir Lancelot led him on a merry dance through the snow, weaving and swaying from the giant's savage attacks. The spectators laughed as each swing of Sir Tarquin's sword hit nothing but thin air.

Fuelled by the crowd's mockery, the giant knight chased faster and swung harder, forcing Sir Lancelot to stand his ground and fight.

Sir Tarquin was powerful, and his blows rained down upon Sir Lancelot's dragon shield like lightning bolts from a thunderstorm.

Bracing his booted feet firmly in the snow, Sir Lancelot withstood the punishing ordeal, waiting for his chance to strike. Yet even though Nimue had purged Sir Roderick's poison from her son's veins, his muscles had not fully recovered, and his energy waned.

Surviving another frenzied assault, Sir Lancelot made his move. As Sir Tarquin pulled back his arm in readiness to unleash another brutal blow, Sir Lancelot spun with whirlwind speed to his right before hammering his blunted blade against the giant's bull-headed helmet. Then, while Sir Tarquin's ears rang, he struck the sword from his gauntleted hand.

Sir Lancelot levelled his blade at Sir Tarquin's throat. 'Do you yield, sir?'

'Never!' Sir Tarquin raged, yanking the helmet from his head and hurling it at Sir Lancelot.

Sir Lancelot sidestepped the speeding bull's head before pointing his sword to where his opponent's blade lay half-submerged in the snow. 'Then we shall fight on.'

Helmetless, Sir Tarquin warily bent to retrieve his sword.

Sir Lancelot now saw the red scar cut into the brute's face. 'Tell me, sir knight,' he said as the two adversaries encircled one another. 'Who gifted you that sweet kiss upon your cheek?'

Sir Tarquin snarled like a wild beast, 'You would be wise to still your flapping tongue!'

The giant lunged, but Sir Lancelot knocked the effort aside.

'Is the scar the reason you seldom remove your helmet? I do not blame you. It is an ugly face. I expect maidens weep and children scream at the sight of you.' By enraging his formidable foe, Sir Lancelot hoped to unbalance him.

Sir Tarquin came again, and once more, Sir Lancelot batted his attacks away with consummate ease.

'I confess,' Sir Lancelot pressed, 'I do not remember your brother. Was he as charming and as handsome as your good self?'

In truth, Sir Lancelot did remember Sir Tarquin's brother, who was every bit as cruel and brutish, and he lost no sleep over the knight's demise.

At the mention of Sir Tarquin's sibling, the brute's fury was rekindled, and he sprung at Sir Lancelot like a man possessed. The ferocity of the attack caught Sir Lancelot off guard, and he quickly found himself defending for his life. The giant knight hacked at him like a butcher chopping meat from bone. Hammer blow after hammer blow crashed against Sir Lancelot's dragon shield. *Now, I must survive the knave's onslaught until he falters.*

Like Sir Galleron before him, Sir Lancelot was bludgeoned onto his knees. He held his shield above his head, absorbing everything the brute threw at him until the painted red dragon was cleaved in two and the wood beneath splintered into kindling.

Sir Tarquin roared. With victory at hand, he channelled all his might into a final assault… Yet, in his eagerness to avenge his brother and end Camelot's returned champion, he lost his footing in the snow.

This was Sir Lancelot's chance. Fast and nimble, he twisted like a cat and smashed Sir Tarquin across his unprotected head using the flat of his blade. The giant spiralled to the ground in a heap.

'Do you yield, sir?' Sir Lancelot demanded a second time.

Fresh blood ran down Sir Tarquin's face, but defiance still burned behind his cruel eyes. However, with his enemy's sword poised to fall, Sir Tarquin had little choice but to concede. 'I yield,' he hissed, spitting the words like bile.

Chapter Eighteen

Treachery

Sir Lancelot du Lac! What a tale to tell the grandchildren. If I am blessed with grandchildren. Edgar had not seen his son for many years, and there was no telling what had befallen him since. He liked to think his boy had met a maiden, married and was growing a family. *Mayhap I'll seek him out and make amends.* He decided life was too short not to make things right between them. The problem with Kiyan was he shared his father's stubborn nature. *He'll listen when I tell him of my friend, Sir Lancelot.*

Champion's Meadow was alive with activity. Knights and their squires came and went. Some returned from their bouts grim-faced and disappointed, while others headed for the arena determined and full of hope. And why not? Three of the favourites had withdrawn from the tournament.

Edgar crossed the white meadow. Many of the pavilions and tents had already vanished, and more were being dismantled as he passed them. *Sore losers and empty purses,* he mused with a wry smile. Seeking glory was an expensive venture.

Edgar ducked inside Sir Lancelot's pavilion and immediately saw something was wrong. 'Thieves,' he cursed. The tent had been ransacked. The tin mirror was on its side, the bed covers strewn about the floor, and the chest in which Sir Lancelot kept his armour and provisions smashed open and its contents pilfered.

The silver-haired veteran hurried to Secace's hiding place and slid his hands inside the pavilion's lining above Sir Lancelot's bed. The sword was gone.

Edgar experienced a sinking sensation. Who else knew where to look? Suddenly, it all made perfect sense. 'Oh, what has he done.' Edgar put his head in his hands and despaired. *Percy has been playing us all along. He is one of Vortimer's brats.* But why ransack the pavilion when he knew where to search? *A feeble attempt at misdirection.*

Had Percy's show of loyalty in the Tipsy Squire been nothing more than an elaborate ploy to gain Sir Lancelot's trust? Sir Roderick had witnessed Secace first-hand that night, and now it seemed Lord Vortimer wanted the sword for himself.

Edgar hastened from the tent. *God's teeth! Sir Lancelot needs that sword!* He and Sir Gawain had set off in pursuit of Sir Tarquin, who had fled Lord Astolat's justice.

With luck, I shall catch Percy before the exchange is made. The veteran was wise to the ways of Astolat's underworld. He had lived in the town long enough to know where the local villains made their deals. *Mostly in dark, dingy haunts far away from prying eyes and wagging tongues.* Moreover, Edgar had friends serving in Lord Astolat's guards who were only too willing to update his knowledge over a tankard of ale.

Where will Percy make the exchange? Somewhere he was familiar with, yet not too remote nor too public. *The Blushing Maiden.*

Located far from the castle and the town's overlooking walls and sentry posts, the inn provided a shadowy haven for crooks and ill-doers alike. The secluded courtyard at the rear of the seedy establishment was a notorious meeting place for thuggery. Not least because Old Dotty, the Maiden's landlady, offered discounted rates to her unsavoury courtyard guests and a promise to watch out for the law while business was conducted.

I'm getting too old for this, Edgar mused, weaving through Astolat's abandoned streets. Everyone else, it seemed, was watching the drama unfold in the arena. The town was deserted, wide-open and lawless—the perfect scenario for skulduggery. What better time was there to undertake a disreputable transaction?

Percy's betrayal had surprised Edgar. There was no questioning that the boy's past was a troubled one, but his future was full of promise. *Squire to Sir Lancelot! What an opportunity.*

'Foolish boy,' the veteran grumbled under his breath. 'I must be losing my touch.' Edgar was gifted with the ability to gauge a man's character, and Percy had passed the test. *Vortimer must have something on the boy*, he reasoned. If the veteran's hunch proved correct, it would better explain Percy's dishonourable deed.

As the Blushing Maiden came into view, Edgar slowed his pace. The inn was a ramshackle establishment with multiple beamed floors stacked haphazardly, one onto another, rearing precariously into the sky, giving the disconcerting impression the building was only one blowy storm from ruin.

Cautiously, Edgar made his way to the rear of the inn via a narrow, ivy-infested side alley. The Blushing Maiden's cobblestoned courtyard was enclosed by moss-covered walls of flint, but many were in ill repair, and gaps between them allowed access to a rambling network of back alleys beyond. Footprints in the snow revealed the popularity of the improvised routes and the frequency with which they were used.

'What are you doing here?' asked a voice.

Startled, Edgar swung around. 'Oh, thank Merlin,' he said with no shortage of relief. 'I'm not too late.'

Percy leant against a young apple tree that protruded from the centre of the courtyard, its bare branches frosted white. 'You should not have come after me,' he said, pushing himself away from the slender trunk.

Edgar saw that Percy carried Secace.

Percy smiled weakly, noting the direction of the veteran's gaze. 'I am truly sorry,' he said, 'but my debts are many.'

'So you thought it a good idea to steal from Sir Lancelot?'

Percy's brow crumpled. 'What are you talking about? I stole from Sir Galaad, as you well know.'

'Sir Galaad is not the Black Knight's true name. He is Sir Lancelot du Lac—King Arthur's lost champion.'

Percy reeled from the news as if struck. 'That explains the sword,' he muttered at last, peering at Secace wrapped in his arms. 'Vortimer craves a sword of power to challenge Excalibur and, with it, overthrow Arthur.' Percy suddenly stared at Edgar with desperate eyes, 'If I do not deliver this weapon to Vortimer, he will kill my mother.'

So, this is Vortimer's hold over the boy. Edgar's features softened. 'It's not too late, Percy. We can find a way. Sir Lancelot will find a way. Come with me. Together, we can save your mother and return the sword.'

Cruel, mocking laughter echoed through the courtyard. Hooded and cloaked in black, figures began emerging between the jagged gaps in the flint walls.

'Oh, I am afraid it is much too late for that,' Lord Vortimer declared. He yanked the cowl from his head, exposing a crown of thick black hair and a smug face twisted with sneering lips and wicked eyes. 'Good work, Percival. Your mother will be pleased.'

Lord Vortimer edged closer toward the boy, his black leather boots crunching through the snow and ice with each deliberate step. Slowly, he reached out with a gloved hand. 'Now, hand me the sword as agreed.'

Edgar drew his blade. 'Don't give it to him, boy,' he said, stepping alongside Percy.

'Look here,' Lord Vortimer announced with amusement. 'The old man wants to play.' Stooping low, he mocked Edgar in front of his men, shuffling across the icy cobblestones with tottering steps. 'Well, let us not deny the old-timer his wishes, my friends.'

Hissing like vipers, swords flew from scabbards.

'I will ask you a second time,' Lord Vortimer said, becoming severe. And by the set of his jaw and the glint in his snake-like eyes, there would be no third time. 'Hand me the sword.'

Edgar counted seven men. Those were not good odds, not even if he were in his prime fighting for King Uther. Edgar could not explain why, but the boy's survival was everything. Percy belonged at Sir Lancelot's side, and by the old gods and the new, he would do everything in his power to make that happen. 'You know what to do, boy,' Edgar said. 'Use the sword!'

Snarling, Lord Vortimer lunged for the weapon held in the youth's grasp.

Shifting aside, Percy slid Sir Lancelot's enchanted blade free, and Secace sang into the frigid air.

Lord Vortimer danced away from the silver weapon, raging with anger. 'Will someone fetch me that forsaken sword!' he demanded, pointing and gesticulating wildly.

Edgar and Percy backed away until they occupied the head of the shadowed alley running alongside the inn. At least here, the enemy could not engage them simultaneously. 'You must take the sword to Sir Lancelot,' Edgar implored. 'Find him, boy. He'll need it.'

Sir Roderick—Lord Vortimer's favourite—commanded his master's soldiers, 'Kill them both and claim the sword!'

Slipping and sliding over the frozen cobblestones, Lord Vortimer's henchmen advanced.

Edgar clashed blades with a burly warrior who pressed the veteran deep into the alley. Percy defended desperately against both Sir Roderick and a lithe, stoat-faced snake. Between them, Lord Vortimer's men overwhelmed the boy, cutting shallow wounds into his arms and legs that stung fiercely. Seeing Percy's plight, Edgar battled his opponent back into the courtyard. He stunned the burly warrior with a thump to the head before slashing his blade across Sir Roderick's thigh.

Sir Roderick emitted a high-pitched scream and stumbled feebly from the fight, leaving the stoat-faced soldier to face Percy alone.

'Swing the damn sword, boy!' Edgar hollered.

Clumsily deflecting the stoat-faced soldier's attack, Percy heaved Secace with all his strength. The snake met the blow with his blade, but the magical sword split the iron-wrought weapon in two before cleaving into flesh. In a spray of scarlet, Stoat Face collapsed into the snow.

Stung by their loss, Lord Vortimer's soldiers pulled back to regroup—but not for long. 'Finish them!' Lord Vortimer cried, encouraging his men forward again. 'I must have that sword!'

'Now run, boy,' Edgar said.

Percy hesitated. 'I cannot leave you to your fate.'

'You must, and you will. You and the sword are more important than the life of an old man. Take your mother to Lord Astolat for protection, then in all haste, catch Sir Lancelot. Now run, boy, and grant me a hero's end.'

Edgar would hold the alley for as long as there was blood in his veins. *If I am going to die, I will die fighting.* And he would take as many of Lord Vortimer's snakes down with him as he could.

'I will not forget you,' Percy pledged. 'Nor will I falter from my path.' Then, with a final glance at Edgar, Percy spun and ran.

'Quickly, kill the old man and follow the sword!' Lord Vortimer ordered.

If only I had found my son before now, Edgar lamented. *Yet, by the gods, I will make Kiyan proud today!*

Grim-faced and defiant, Edgar gripped his longsword with both hands. 'You best go back through the wall because you'll not go through me!'

Chapter Nineteen

The Sword of Shining

Nine riders splashed through the shallow waters of a stream. Powering up the river's muddy bank, they climbed a grassy slope before disappearing into a sprawling expanse of dark, dense woodland.

Sir Lancelot and his knights had tailed Sir Tarquin west, tracking him through icy valleys, across frozen lakes, and over rolling hills of white. The riders kept their distance, not wanting to spook the brute. Nonetheless, with the forest in sight, Sir Tarquin had bolted like a hare with the scent of wolf in its nostrils.

The knights reeled in their prey deep within the forest, thundering through the trees at a canter amongst the twisting branches and knotted boughs. No longer was their presence in doubt. Perhaps the brute had always known and was leading his pursuers precisely where he wanted them to be. Even so, they had little choice but to follow.

The path through the trees narrowed, forcing Sir Lancelot and his knights to ride one after another. The sharp, barren branches of the forest lashed them as they passed, almost as if the trees sought to knock them from their mounts.

Somewhere amidst the shadowy woodland, Sir Lancelot was convinced they would find Morgana's lair and, gods willing, Albion's queen locked inside. 'I am coming, Guinevere,' he whispered into the rushing wind.

The chase gathered pace, and the pack closed in. Astride Cedric, Sir Lancelot led the charge. In the Black Knight's wake galloped Sir Gawain, Sir Lavaine, and Lord Astolat's finest knights, Sir Ector, Sir Rillius, Sir Ghyll, Sir Bevos, Sir Brin, and Sir Arkus.

Sir Tarquin was within their reach, the brute's midnight stallion pounding the forest path ahead. 'Stay on the knave!' Sir Lancelot bellowed, determined to chase the giant knight to the gates of his master's lair.

Yet beyond reason, Sir Tarquin promptly vanished, and the day suddenly darkened as if night had come too soon.

'What cursed sorcery is this?' Sir Gawain cried. Gazing upwards, he saw the sky cloaked by the tangled branches of the woodland trees.

The knights reined their skittish mounts to a halt. Cedric reared high into the air, hooves whirling. Oak, ash, and elm blocked their path, their crooked limbs entwined.

'The trees move,' Sir Lavaine declared, horrified. 'The forest conspires against us!'

The knights scarcely believed their eyes. The mighty trees remained rooted to the spot, but their branches bent and swayed with menace.

'Arm yourselves!' Sir Lancelot yelled, drawing his sword.

'Do we retreat and find another route?' Sir Lavaine questioned breathlessly. The leafless branches had woven themselves into a seemingly impenetrable barrier.

Sir Ghyll wheeled his mare around. 'It is too late to go back,' he declared hopelessly. 'The forest seals us inside its dark domain!'

Sir Lancelot shifted his mount to see. Sir Ghyll spoke the truth; the trees wrapped their branches together here, too. There was no escape.

'A trap!' Sir Gawain growled.

Sir Lancelot grimaced. *Sir Gawain is right. Sir Tarquin knowingly led us here to our doom.* Confirming his fears, Nimue's enchanted ring pulsed blue around his neck. 'We are at the sufferance of Morgana's witchcraft,' he cautioned. 'We must force passage with might and muscle before the witch's magic destroys us.'

'So be it,' Sir Gawain replied grimly. The brave knight dug his booted heels into the flanks of his charger and thundered into the heart of the cursed grove. Camelot's champion hacked with his sword, chopping through the smaller branches with ease, but against the larger limbs, his blade was useless.

Creepers and vines shot from the undergrowth, binding themselves around Sir Gawain's sword arm. The snake-like crawlers tightened their barbed grip until the knight's blade tumbled into the snow. 'Mercy! I am caught!'

Sir Lancelot stared aghast as the trees attacked. Boughs swung like vast clubs, and branches lunged like giant spears. From beneath the pawing hooves of the knights' terrified horses, roots, twisted and gnarled, burst from the frozen earth, ensnaring arms and legs within their iron-like clutches. And now, with Sir Lancelot's knights helpless, Morgana's woodland army set about its deadly work.

Sir Ghyll was the first to perish. He could do nothing save watch and wail as the flailing branches of a mighty oak lashed him ragged.

Creepers wormed their way through mail and leather before piercing skin and flesh. The vengeful forest consumed the knight's screams, muffling them until they were no louder than incoherent murmurings of misery.

Even if we cut free, there is nowhere to run, nowhere to hide, Sir Lavaine despaired.

As the trees tightened their grip, the sky darkened further, an all-encompassing gloom, ghastly and grim. The knights hung motionless, awaiting the enchanted forest's malevolent will. Hope was fading.

'Courage, men!' Sir Gawain bellowed. But finding courage in the face of death when there was no hope of altering the inevitability of its coming was not easy.

Sir Bevos was next to meet a grisly end. Pulled limb from limb, the knight's screams were terrible to endure. Sir Lancelot cast his eyes to the ground, unable to watch the awful sight.

To fail Guinevere in this way was a dagger through Sir Lancelot's heart. Yet, thanks to Nimue's ring, he alone was free from the forest's curse. He butchered the creepers wrapped around Sir Gawain's arms and legs, but for every vine hacked to the snow, another sprung forth, taking its place.

Soon, the trees were crashing their branches against Sir Lancelot's shimmering blue shield, doing their utmost to crush him deep into the soil. But try as they might, the forest could not break Nimue's magic. *Yet, for how long will my mother's shield hold?* And how long before he and his knights were ripped to pieces and strewn across the forest floor like Sir Bevos?

A second light illuminated the darkness. *It shines from behind the cursed wall,* Sir Lancelot observed. Like Nimue's ring, it gleamed with an unnatural glare, not blue but a brilliant silver. The light pulsed again and again, growing brighter and brighter. Then, a shimmering blade slashed through bark and branch, shattering the barrier and bathing all beyond in silver.

The roots and creepers holding the knights receded at once, and the trees bent away, cowering from the glare like vampires from the sun.

Silhouetted amidst the light was a man.

'Sir Lancelot, take your sword!'

Reaching out, Sir Lancelot claimed his enchanted blade from Percy's grasp. 'The Sword of Shining!'

In a whirlwind of blazing silver, Sir Lancelot carved the barricade of oak, ash, and elm into splinters, breaking the witch's spell.

'Now we ride!' Sir Lancelot cried.

Chapter Twenty

The Black Tower

The knights powered their warhorses through the shattered remains of Morgana's trap, galloping in reckless haste to leave the terrible scene far behind them.

In time, they slowed to gather their wits.

'The witch's magic has grown strong indeed if she can bend the trees of the forest to her will,' Sir Lavaine stated gravely.

True enough, Sir Lancelot mused. *If not for Secace, our fate would be sealed, our limbs torn from our bodies.* He grimaced at the dreadful image of Sir Bevos being pulled apart by roots and creepers.

'How did you find us?' Sir Lancelot asked Percy. The young man had hardly said a word since his timely intervention.

Percy met Sir Lancelot's gaze with troubled eyes. 'A blackbird,' he answered. 'I know it sounds strange, but I swear it is the truth.'

Despite the horrors of the cursed wood, Sir Lancelot smiled. 'I believe you.' He might have guessed his mother was involved. They owed her their lives. Yet the squire's bleak demeanour concerned the knight. 'What happened, Percy? Where is Edgar?'

Percy's face dropped further. 'I betrayed him… and you,' he muttered wretchedly. 'I stole Secace on Vortimer's request. Edgar tried to stop me, and now he is dead.'

The news of Edgar's demise saddened Sir Lancelot. The wily veteran had proved a steadfast companion during the short time he had known him. Sir Lancelot guessed there was more to the incident than Percy was saying, but the knight held his tongue until the tale was freely told in full. In Sir Lancelot's experience, pressing a man seldom reaped answers.

Beneath the creaking branches of the forest, the pair rode in silence for a time, but it wasn't long before Percy felt compelled to unburden his soul. 'The sword was the price for my mother's life,' he said quietly. 'Edgar begged me to come to you for help. But it was too late.' Overwhelmed with shame, the young man cast his eyes down to the ground.

'Yet return the sword you did. And without doing so, all would be lost.' Sir Lancelot nudged Cedric onwards toward Sir Gawain, leaving Percy alone. The boy needed time and space to face his failings without the meddlesome questioning of others.

'The forest grows thin,' Sir Gawain observed, staring into the deepening gloom. 'Look,' the knight raised a gauntleted hand and pointed into the distance where a dark shape revealed itself between the trees. 'See there, a tower rising into the sky?'

Under the unblinking gaze of the luminous moon, Sir Lancelot and his knights emerged from the forest into a glade. Here, the snow lay thick, knee-deep or more in places—a vast white shroud enveloping the land. The warhorses ploughed a yawning furrow through the glistening terrain, winding their way toward the black tower looming high above. The structure reared into the night like a sentinel from the Otherworld, a baleful stone giant, ominous and ever watchful.

Sir Lancelot recalled Hellawes' prophecy: *Guinevere resides in the west... A castle in the wild woods.*

From the highest window, a flickering light promised life within. *Guinevere?* Was Camelot's queen to be found at the top of this granite monster? And what of Morgana and her minions? What of Sir Tarquin?

'Be on your guard, men,' Sir Lancelot advised. 'If the witch resides within, she will be wise to our arrival.'

'Yet what of her henchmen?' Sir Lavaine questioned. Not a soul stirred except for the knights and their snorting mounts. 'The place is abandoned. See how the snow lies undisturbed?'

'Then what of the light?' Sir Gawain argued. He eyed their surroundings with suspicion, expecting Morgana to unleash another attack at any moment. 'Covering footprints in the snow is child's play for a devil witch such as she.'

Securing their steeds to the stump of a fallen tree, its decaying bark frozen white with frost, the knights resumed on foot, wading through the snow to the tower's black gates. Wasting no time, Sir Gawain shouldered the oaken door but without success. 'The way is barred,' he announced, preparing himself for a second charge.

Sir Lancelot drew his sword. 'Stand aside, Sir Gawain.' *If Secace can split trunks in two, a wooden gate will prove no less demanding.*

Mustering all his strength, Sir Lancelot crashed the Sword of Shining against the blackened oak. A searing flash dazzled their eyes, and an explosion of splintered wood deafened their ears. If Morgana was inside, now their existence was undoubtedly revealed.

Once the dust settled, the knights brandished their blades and stepped over the broken timber into the shadowed hall beyond. Expecting resistance, they were met only with empty blackness.

Sir Lancelot moved deeper inside, Secace illuminating the darkest of corners. There was a chill within the dark tower, surpassing even the cold felt outside in the snow-covered glade.

'There is no one here,' Sir Lavaine whispered, his breath a swirling mist in the cold still air.

'We shall see,' Sir Lancelot said.

The Sword of Shining's intense light faded to a pale sheen, and by the weapon's glow, the knights quickly found a stairwell twisting both up and down.

'Which way?' Sir Gawain queried.

Beneath them was a black hole, a stairway to nothingness. From its depths, there rose a rank odour. 'We go up,' Sir Lancelot announced, drawn by the light spilling from the high window.

Sir Lavaine and two knights of Astolat, Sir Ector and Sir Rillius, remained behind in the hall. 'If events turn awry, we shall be ready to guard your retreat,' King Pelles' son declared.

'You, too, Percy,' Sir Lancelot instructed. 'Stay with Sir Lavaine and prepare for our return.' The boy was untrained and would be susceptible to an untimely end if trouble found them and battle was joined.

Two abreast, the knights clambered up the stone stairs. The light beckoned them upwards, and with each step gained, its brightness strengthened. Ignoring all but the last level, where the way ended atop the tower's fortified summit, they ducked into a narrow passage. At its end, past shadowed openings, there stood a door. A golden beam lanced into the passageway from the chamber beyond like sunrise glinting through woodland trees. Here was the source of the dark tower's radiance.

Traversing the length of the corridor, Sir Lancelot thumped the door with a gauntleted fist, the noise a resounding drumbeat that seemed to reverberate through every inch of the tower. 'Queen Guinevere?'

There was no reply.

'Guinevere, it is I, Sir Lancelot,' he called softly. 'If you can hear me, stand well clear.' Once more, he swung Secace, smashing the timber asunder with a crashing roar.

Inside the chamber, huddled against the far wall beneath a barred window revealing the moonlit night beyond, was a raven-haired woman. She appeared worn and weary with tangled hair and a body as thin as a reed, yet she was still beautiful with gleaming eyes of green.

'Guinevere!' Sir Lancelot cried.

Gasping in shock, Guinevere's hands covered her face. Tears of joy streamed from her eyes. 'Can it really be true after all this time? I pray you are not another of Morgana's tricks?'

'We are real enough, I promise.' Sir Lancelot wanted nothing more than to run to Guinevere and wrap his arms around her, but with Sir Gawain behind him, he held his emotions in check. 'Has Morgana harmed you?' he asked instead.

'No, but I have been alone for so long, I feared losing my mind.'

'You have my apologies, my Queen. Day and night, Arthur's knights have searched the length and breadth of Albion for you.'

Guinevere smiled. 'And thank the old gods and the new, now you have found me.'

Sir Gawain bowed before Guinevere. 'Where is the witch, my Queen?'

In his relief and elation, Sir Lancelot had forgotten Guinevere's captors. He tore his gaze from her emerald eyes, trying to focus his mind. Their quest was incomplete until Arthur's queen was safely escorted back to Camelot.

'Morgana and Mellegrans rode out this morning. I saw them from my window. I do not know their destination.'

Sir Lancelot praised their good fortune. 'Then let us be away before their return.'

'What of your knights, my Queen?' Sir Gawain pressed. 'What has the witch done with them?'

Guinevere looked heartbroken. 'I fear they are lost. Their screams haunt my nights, but of late, there has only been silence.' She peered into Sir Gawain's eyes with renewed hope. 'You must check the dungeons. Perchance they live, however unlikely as it seems.'

Sir Gawain bowed once more. 'I shall see it done, my Queen.' He faced Sir Lancelot. 'We shall await you by the mounts.' Without delay, Sir Gawain rushed from the chamber. 'Sir Brin, Sir Arkus, with me!'

Alone, Sir Lancelot and Guinevere embraced.

'I have missed you so. More than you will ever know,' Guinevere whispered, brushing the knight's cheek with her lips. 'I prayed you would come. Over and over, from sunup to sundown and during the everlasting night in between.'

Gently withdrawing from Guinevere's arms, Sir Lancelot held her hands and stared into her beautiful eyes. 'And who did you pray to?' he asked softly. 'To the old gods or the new? Or to the dark gods of the Otherworld far beneath the earth?'

A moment of confusion contorted Guinevere's features, but then her eyes narrowed in understanding. A ring tied around Sir Lancelot's neck pulsed blue. *Nimue's magic.*

'No, wait!'

Tightening his hold of Guinevere with his left hand, Sir Lancelot thrust Secace into her belly with his right. The queen shrieked in anguish, and as the knight pushed his blade deeper inside her body, her screams sang through the frozen tower like the chilling cries of a banshee. 'Where is Guinevere, foul witch?'

Guinevere howled like a wounded animal. She writhed against Sir Lancelot's enchanted sword, unable to separate herself from its cold embrace. Her face blurred, bulging and shifting, changing until she was the queen no longer.

'Where is she?'

Morgana spat blood-streaked sputum into the knight's dark eyes. 'Rot in death!'

'Tell me!' Sir Lancelot levered Secace up and down inside the witch's guts.

Fresh screams of torment exploded from Morgana's lungs. 'She is atop the tower,' she moaned. 'Contained within a cell upon the summit. Please, have mercy, I beg you. Lord Mellegrans forced my obedience. I am innocent!'

'Your lies are poison, witch! What did you hope to accomplish by your deception?' Sir Lancelot hissed. 'It matters not. The sentence for your wickedness is death.' Sir Lancelot ripped Secace from Morgana's innards, but before the knight administered the telling blow, the witch cast her spells against him.

A wailing wind struck Sir Lancelot. Morgana hurled the knight into the corridor and slammed him headlong against the wall opposite the chamber. Despite her eagerness to see Sir Lancelot dead, the witch fell to her knees. 'You will not escape this tower… or my wrath!' she wailed, desperately trying to hold her squirming guts inside her body.

Gathering himself, Sir Lancelot held his shining sword before him and made for the stairs, fleeing Morgana's vengeance. *I must find Guinevere.*

Chapter Twenty-One

Morgana's Wrath

Sir Gawain and his knights clattered down the steps, delving into the deepest depths of the tower, the air ranker the further they sank.

'Be on your guard, men. Evil lingers here. I can feel it in my bones,' Sir Gawain warned, repelled by the sickly aroma below.

The tight stairwell ended before a barred but unlocked gate. Pushing the gate open, Camelot's champion was presented with a wall of impenetrable darkness. He fumbled inside, exploring the grim chamber as well as he could manage, blindly feeling with his hands. If the ghastly place had once harboured prisoners, they had long since departed, dead or alive.

'Come, there is nothing here but the scent of death.'

High above, the tormented screams of a woman shattered the silence—a spine-tingling wail to freeze the blood and still the heart. Soon after, the glow of torchlight graced the dungeons, spilling from the hall above.

Sir Arkus and Sir Brin mounted the stairs to investigate.

'Wait,' Sir Gawain whispered. A wavering orange shard highlighted a shape slumped in the furthest corner of the gaol. 'A knight!'

Sir Gawain rushed to the figure's side. A man stared blankly into nothingness, his face battered and bloodied. 'Alas, Sir Agravain.'

*

Sir Lavaine swept aside a savage swipe. Then, stumbling backwards, he parried a lunge from a second blade. The enemy had appeared from nowhere, materialising from the shadows like ghosts from the Otherworld. They burst forward, brandishing sharp swords and flaming torches, hollering battle cries with the look of murder in their eyes.

'Rally to me!' Sir Lavaine called.

Slashing and slicing, Percy forced his way to Sir Lavaine's side, but Sir Ector and Sir Rillius were waylaid by a host of foes and forced to fight for their lives where they stood.

The enemy knights bore the markings of King Bagdemagus—three grey watchtowers. *Of which, presumably, this ancient stronghold is one*, Sir Lavaine mused. *So, Morgana's ally is revealed*. In truth, the union made perfect sense, a match well-suited. Both shared a common adversary in Arthur, even if, until now, only one—his estranged sister—had openly declared their villainy for the high king.

'What do we do?' Percy cried. He wielded his sword two-handed, hacking wildly, frantically trying to keep the enemy at arm's length. Without armour or shield, he could ill-afford an opponent penetrating his defences.

'Against all the odds, we must reclaim the stairwell!'

Percy despaired. 'There must be a dozen men between us and there!'

'We need to reunite with Sir Ector and Sir Rillius,' Sir Lavaine said. Only together could such a daring sortie be accomplished.

However, that hope was promptly snatched from Sir Lavaine's grasp.

The Tower Knights pressed for the kill. Sir Rillius quickly fell to a sword thrust through the heart, and Sir Ector was wounded when a lancing sword escaped the knight's guard to puncture a thigh. Percy faltered, too. He swung his sword with ever-decreasing potency, knowing he would be a dead man if he were to stop.

Sir Lavaine deflected an axe against his shield before skewering a Tower Knight through the neck. Yet even as the man's corpse sank to the cold stone floor, Sir Lavaine was assailed by a screaming swarm of grey and green knights intent on inflicting his swift demise.

Suddenly, a bellowing battle cry boomed through the hall, and a glinting blade whirled and fell in the gloom. Drawn to the stairwell, the Tower Knights massed for a counterattack.

'Sir Gawain!' Sir Lavaine yelled. 'By Bran's beard, here is Arthur's champion to save us!'

Flanked by Sir Brin and Sir Arkus, Sir Gawain fell upon the enemy line like a raging tempest, cleaving foes to the floor in their droves. 'Sir Lavaine,' Sir Gawain called, 'we must fight our way to the top of the tower. Sir Lancelot is in grave danger!'

*

Negotiating the passageway, Sir Lancelot surged up the stairwell and out into the moonlit night atop the tower. 'Guinevere!' he yelled, spinning and twisting, desperately searching.

A muffled cry answered, 'I am here!'

Sir Lancelot hurried across the icy platform toward the sound of Guinevere's voice. Concealed behind the snow-laden stonework housing the stairwell, he found Albion's lost queen chained inside a cage fit only for an animal.

Sir Lancelot was mortified by Guinevere's appearance. Bedraggled and frail, she was a shadow of her former glory. 'What has she done to you?' he whispered, unable to disguise the horror from his voice.

Guinevere gripped her cage with dirt-stained fingers and stared between the bars at the grim-faced knight peering at her. 'Lancelot? Is it you who stands before me?' she rasped. 'Or do my eyes deceive me?'

Sir Lancelot placed his gauntleted hands on hers. 'Your eyes see true, my Queen,' he said. 'I have come to take you home.'

Relieved beyond measure, Guinevere sagged against the bars of the cage, 'Thank the gods.' She raised her head, and with eyes glistening with tears, she smiled. 'Rescue me, my brave Sir Lancelot, and may I never set foot within this cursed tower again.'

Wielding Secace, Sir Lancelot smote the cage in two. Then, reaching inside, he helped his queen from her prison.

Gingerly, Guinevere straightened her limbs. Having spent so long cramped within the confined space, her body had grown crooked.

'Can you walk?'

Guinevere stumbled into Sir Lancelot's arms.

'Not well, it seems,' he said, sweeping her into the air. 'Our circumstances are dire, my Queen. We must flee this place at once. Morgana yet lives,' he explained before she protested against being slung over his shoulder like a sack of grain.

Too feeble to argue, Guinevere clasped her hands around Sir Lancelot's neck and held on tightly. Yet their escape was halted before it was begun.

'I will not be deprived of my prize,' Morgana le Fay hissed. 'Nor my chance to usurp my brother's throne.' Escorted by Lord Mellegrans and her Dark Knights, the witch confronted them atop the high tower beneath the pale moon and a black, fathomless sky.

Gently, Sir Lancelot placed Guinevere onto her feet. 'Stay behind me,' he said, drawing Secace.

Morgana shoved aside Lord Mellegrans' supporting arm, her grievous wound forgotten. 'Nimue's magic will not save you this time, fool. Now, you will witness the full extent of my master's power.'

Morgana flew into a rage, her green eyes ablaze with fury. She held her hands high into the night sky and screamed strange words into the rising wind.

I must stop her before she casts her spells. Lofting Secace into the air, Sir Lancelot rushed the witch, determined to cleave her from neck to navel.

A blast of wavering lightning crackled from Morgana's outstretched hands. Nimue's ring flared blue, neutralising the dancing red energy threatening to engulf and destroy Sir Lancelot.

Unchecked by the witch's spell, Sir Lancelot advanced.

Morgana let fly with another bout of devilry, this time directing her dark magic not at Sir Lancelot himself but at the shimmering sword held above his head. Red lightning tore the knight's enchanted blade from his grasp, sweeping the weapon high into the howling wind and casting it into the waiting darkness beyond the tower.

Sir Lancelot and Guinevere backed away from Morgana's wrath until they were pressed hard against the tower's ramparts. Camelot's queen clasped Sir Lancelot's hands, 'I would rather leap to my doom than spend a moment longer in the witch's clutches.'

'Do not think it,' Sir Lancelot demanded passionately. 'Whilst there is breath in my body, I will defend you.' Yet save for the protection gleaned from his mother's magic ring, he was unarmed and could not think how he might prevent Guinevere's recapture.

Morgana sneered. 'How very touching. Star-crossed lovers destined for ruin. You betray my brother as equally as I.' Edging closer, the witch's hands rose once more. 'And now, brave Sir Lancelot, you will perish.'

A torrent of red lightning burst from Morgana's fingertips. The infernal energy roared through the crisp winter air like an electrical monster wrought from pure evil, illuminating the watchtower's summit with a flickering storm of crimson flashes.

As before, Nimue's magic ring came to the knight's aid—a pulsing luminous shield of blue. The witch's lightning broke upon its surface as harmlessly as waves crashing against the shore. Morgana channelled more and more of the dark, destructive magic toward him—a relentless flow of red-hot power. Yet the blue shield held.

Exhausted, Morgana lowered her hands. A foul, pungent smoke lay heavy atop the tower. Sir Lancelot's protective sphere dissipated. Yet, the ordeal was far from over.

'Curse your mother!' Morgana screamed. The witch began chanting again, faster and louder than before. Hot breath billowed from her lips, rising into the icy air before being borne away on gusting winds.

Lord Mellegrans stepped from Morgana's side. Crazed by power, the witch's devotion to the dark arts had gone too far, and he had no wish to witness the results. He distanced himself from Morgana's dreadful ranks, shuddering at the sight of the woman's Dark Knights. Unmoving, they remained dutifully lined behind their mistress, ready to do her bidding.

Sir Lancelot withdrew beside his queen, praying his mother's magic continued to thwart Morgana.

'Take heart,' Guinevere encouraged. 'If nothing else, we have hope.'

Huddled at the edge of the tower, Sir Lancelot held Guinevere close. Above them, the starlit sky was split asunder. A peel of apocalyptic thunder cracked the heavens. Peering upwards, Sir Lancelot saw a giant fiery rift in the night, and from its flaming heart, it disgorged writhing black shadows that wailed like death itself.

Lord Mellegrans scrambled inside Guinevere's empty cage, 'The demons are coming! The demons are coming!' Tormented by the dreadful sight, he curled into a ball before whimpering and snivelling.

Guinevere, too, was overcome by fear, 'What devilry is this? The witch has called forth the spirits of the Otherworld to claim our souls. We must jump before they take us all to Hell!' Guinevere could not tear her eyes from the terrifying entities descending from the blazing sky.

'No,' Sir Lancelot stated resolutely. 'We fight.' He unslung his shield and took Guinevere's hand.

Suddenly, the tower top was plunged into mayhem. Fighting a running battle, knights flooded onto the summit from the stairwell. Grey and green versus red and silver.

'What is happening?' Morgana shrieked. 'Mellegrans! Where are you, worm?' Amidst the madness, she lost control of her wraiths. The things circled overhead like monstrous bats, plummeting from the night sky to snatch screaming men from the tower.

'Now we run!' Sir Lancelot used his shield to hammer the witch into the snow while she was distracted. Then, as Morgana's Dark Knights lurched into life, forming a protective ring around their fallen mistress, he snatched up a discarded sword beside the body of a fallen Tower Knight and fled with Guinevere into the chaos.

Chapter Twenty-Two

The Renegade Knight

A part of Sir Kay had awoken. He remembered who he was and what he had become. The sight of Guinevere in peril had stirred his soul, or whatever it was that still endured inside his ravaged body.

Sir Kay was unsure whether he lived or not, but the despair consuming his every moment was now overcome by a desperate desire to protect Camelot's queen.

The sky was on fire, yet through his blood-red eyes, the world was nothing but shadow. Amidst the black fog clouding his thoughts, he saw his creator as clearly as if she were lit beneath the rising sun, the witch responsible for his miserable half-life. *She will pay for what she has done.*

Sir Kay loomed over her, his blade ready to end her despicable existence. The witch cowered away, scrabbling backwards through the snow and ice. *You cannot run from justice.*

Sir Kay struck down with deadly force… but with a jarring clang, his iron blade hit metal.

Another of Morgana's creations had saved her, blocking Sir Kay's sword with its own. *Sir Ladinas.* The wretch remained cursed by the witch's spell, and he defended his mistress' life with what was left of his own.

The two knights clashed swords atop the tower—once stout comrades, now fierce enemies. Their black blades hacked and sliced one another's bodies, but neither warrior bled or felt pain.

The witch is too well-guarded. I must protect my queen.

Dropping his sword, Sir Kay shouldered Sir Ladinas against the battlements.

Sir Ladinas was pinned between rough stone and his foe but somehow managed to sink his blade deep inside Sir Kay's body, lancing through ribs and lungs.

Despite the metal jutting from his torso and the blood bubbling from his lips, Sir Kay heaved his corrupted comrade into the air. 'Forgive me,' he whispered before throwing Sir Ladinas into darkness.

*

Morgana was spent. She lay amidst the snow, barely able to move. The power required to summon such fearsome creatures was beyond anything she had channelled before, and the experience had drained her to within an inch of her life. Above, the unearthly portal began to close, the wraiths withdrawing from whence they came, returning to the fiery depths of the Otherworld with a bounty of souls.

Morgana felt for her wound. The gruesome injury had all but healed, yet her insides churned and seethed like boiling pitch. 'Curse him!' she hissed. 'Curse them all!'

Even now, Sir Lancelot and Guinevere were trying to escape the tower. Morgana eyed her Dark Knights. Grim-faced and statue-still, they stood over her, guarding her like human gargoyles. Not all was lost... not yet.

*

Gutting a Tower Knight, Sir Lancelot twisted to face another. He stopped a flailing mace against his shield before dispatching the bearded soldier with a thrust through the guts.

Guinevere kept behind Sir Lancelot, ducking and diving from groping hands, swinging swords, and swooping wraiths. 'Have mercy!' she cried. 'How are we to reach freedom when our path is blighted with so many enemies?'

'Down!' Sir Lancelot pulled Guinevere into the snow. A blur of movement streaked overhead. A Tower Knight poised to smash Sir Lancelot with his axe was swept skyward.

'Fear not, my Queen,' Sir Lancelot said. 'The enemy's appetite for battle wears thin—at least those who are human.'

The things pounced from above repeatedly, plucking soldiers from the tower and returning with them into the rift. Soon enough, Lord Mellegrans' men fled for their souls, hurling themselves headfirst down the stairwell while their lord cowered inside Guinevere's cage like a frightened child.

Heartened by the enemy's retreat, Sir Lancelot and Guinevere joined their fleeing ranks. Lord Mellegrans' soldiers paid little heed. The fight was gone from them. They only wanted to be free from the forsaken tower as fast as possible.

'We must hurry, Morgana's knights approach,' Guinevere stated anxiously, glancing back over her shoulder. 'When will the witch leave us be?'

'When I am dead, and you are retaken,' Sir Lancelot muttered darkly. He saw the truth of Guinevere's warning. Four black-clad brutes with blades drawn and red eyes blazing trudged across the tower straight for them. Sir Lancelot did not have the heart to reveal the horrible truth of their origins to Guinevere, although he guessed she harboured suspicions. They were terrible enough without knowing who they once were.

I have no choice but to confront them, Sir Lancelot thought bleakly. He and Guinevere were going nowhere until the Tower Knights cleared the stairwell. Secace was gone, but Camelot's greatest champion was not easily bested—with or without enchanted swords.

Sir Lancelot spun and faced Morgana's monsters. Sir Gawain and the last of the knights—Sir Lavaine, Sir Ector, and Sir Arkus—joined him. Sir Brin had fallen prey to a wraith, and Percy had long since been dispatched to ready the horses. The heart of battle was no place for an untrained squire.

The moon above was tainted red with the scarlet flames of the rift. The portal to the Otherworld had closed, but its fiery glow lingered. Under the eerie sky, Morgana's red-eyed creatures attacked Sir Lancelot's knights, and the ringing of metal sang into the night.

Sir Lancelot opened his opponent's belly, but neither did the knight flinch or falter. Instead, the black armoured monster hammered its blade against Sir Lancelot's shield.

Sir Gawain slashed a Dark Knight wide-open, but the thing fought on as if the wound was nothing more than a graze. Sir Lavaine clove his blade deep into a monster's torso, Sir Ector slit open another's gullet, and Sir Arkus gutted a fourth like a fish—yet the creatures were seemingly unaffected by pain or injury.

'Go, Sir Lancelot!' Sir Gawain said, parrying a Dark Knight's sword. 'Take the queen and flee. We will hold them.'

A rain of savage blows pummelled Sir Lancelot's shield into oblivion. Tossing it aside, he smashed his sword against the Dark Knight's helmet, forcing the monster away. Quickly, Sir Lancelot grabbed Guinevere's hand, pulling her into the stairwell. The last of Lord Mellegrans' men vanished ahead of them as the pair fled the tower in the enemy's wake.

Atop the summit, Morgana's grim creations pushed Sir Gawain and the knights ever backwards. 'Hold!' he thundered. They needed to give Sir Lancelot and Guinevere more time. Beside him, Sir Arkus fell to a thrusting black blade, and moments later, Sir Ector shared his comrade's fate when he was skewered through the chest like a boar.

'Another foe joins the fray!' Sir Lavaine wailed.

A fifth Dark Knight approached to seal their doom.

'Courage, Sir Lavaine,' Sir Gawain cried, eyeing the monster with dread. It joined its cursed brethren, its inhuman gaze burning like wildfire.

The ungodly warrior swung its black blade two-handed, a blow to slay a dragon. The sword arced through the night like the Grim Reaper's scythe, whistling past Sir Gawain and Sir Lavaine to strike the head from a Dark Knight's shoulders.

'By Bran's beard,' Sir Gawain murmured disbelievingly. 'They fight each other!'

'Praise be,' Sir Lavaine gasped. Seeing Sir Arkus and Sir Ector's demise, the knight had thought it only a matter of time before he joined them crumpled at the enemy's feet.

Sir Kay butchered a second Dark Knight into the snow, hewing its limbs from its torso one after the other. *We cannot be killed, but we can be stopped.*

Morgana's red-eyed monsters swung to engage the renegade knight, sparing Sir Gawain and Sir Lavaine.

'Now is our chance!' Sir Gawain cried. 'Let us flee!'

As Sir Gawain and Sir Lavaine turned to escape, the renegade knight's battle cry thundered across the tower behind them, 'For Camelot!'

*

Sir Lancelot and Guinevere burst through the splintered black gate and out into the snow-shrouded clearing.

'The horses are close,' Sir Lancelot encouraged, leading Guinevere from the tower. 'But we must hurry.'

'Patience. I cannot keep up,' Guinevere protested, stumbling through the drifts.

Reaching the mounts, Sir Lancelot hoisted Guinevere into the air, placing the queen onto Cedric's back. 'We will be away soon enough,' he promised, unlooping the warhorse's reins from the tree stump. Sir Lancelot loathed abandoning his comrades in battle, but Guinevere was everything. Nothing mattered more to Albion than Camelot's queen. *And nothing matters more to me than Guinevere.*

Cedric became skittish, tossing his head and snorting. Guinevere soothed the animal, stroking his flank. 'Sssshhh… We are leaving now.' *This cursed place unnerves him.* It had certainly unnerved her. Never had she witnessed nightmares come to life. *Morgana must be stopped.* But that was a task for another day; escaping her clutches was enough for now.

Suddenly, Cedric reared into the air, kicking out with his hooves. Guinevere grabbed the animal's mane and held on. She saw movement in the shadows. 'Watch out!' she warned Sir Lancelot.

A huge figure loomed from the darkness. 'For my brother!' Sir Tarquin bellowed, lashing at Sir Lancelot with his longsword.

As fast as he was, Sir Lancelot could not counter the brute's blade, at least not entirely. Twisting away, the weapon caught him a glancing blow to the ribs, knocking the air from his lungs and the strength from his limbs. Stunned, Sir Lancelot was at his enemy's mercy.

Sir Tarquin grinned darkly. 'I will enjoy this,' he said, raising his blade high over his head, ready to finish his nemesis once and for all.

'No!' Guinevere screamed. She tugged Cedric's reins, desperately trying to turn the warhorse so he might flail the knave with his hooves. But she was too late.

Sir Tarquin's sword fell… Yet the blade failed to bite into Sir Lancelot's flesh. Instead, the weapon plunged harmlessly into the snow while the brute's scarred face contorted with agony.

'Look!' Guinevere gasped.

A shining sword protruded from the giant's chest, the blade gleaming like the stars in the sky.

Sir Tarquin of Tallyhorn's corpse slid from the enchanted weapon and toppled face-first into the white snow beside Sir Lancelot. Behind them, with Secace clasped in his hands, stood Percy.

*

Morgana hauled herself to her feet and slumped against the crenellations, holding onto the cold stone for support. Beneath the blood-red sky, she gazed from the tower to see her precious prize escaping.

'You have failed,' Lord Mellegrans declared. Only once the wraiths had disappeared into the rift and the fighting had ceased had he crawled from his cage to rejoin the witch's side.

Morgana quivered with rage. 'It is you who has failed, Mellegrans. Was it not your knight's folly that led our enemies to our gates?' The witch seethed, but she contained the urge to punish the fool. Lord Mellegrans still had his uses. 'With more time, my plans would have flourished. Now they burn. Yet we must not despair. Like the phoenix, we must rise from the ashes.'

Morgana watched Sir Lancelot ride into the tree line. Guinevere shared the knight's saddle. She clung to him, her arms wrapped tight, her body pressed close.

Morgana le Fay smiled, her emerald eyes burning with zeal. 'The irony of it all,' she whispered. 'In my stead, Arthur's queen will accomplish my work for me, and I shall be at hand when my brother's kingdom crumbles around him, pulled down from within, piece by piece. I have not lost. I have won.'

Epilogue

King for a Day

The bells of Camelot rang with joyous thunder, a triumphant chant echoing through every corridor, chamber, and hall. Vast red dragon banners billowed from the castle's gleaming white towers. The high king and his knights were finally home. The war was won. The invaders smashed back across the sea.

A year had passed since the queen's abduction, and now Guinevere sat by Arthur's side bedecked in sparkling jewels and feast day finery, the memory of her awful incarceration nothing but a terrible dream.

Dressed in white and draped in red, Percy knelt before the throne. 'In the presence of my king and all those gathered here today, I promise to uphold the knight's code—honour, truth, valour, and loyalty.'

The high king drew his sword. 'By the power of Excalibur, I name you a Knight of Camelot.' Using the flat of his magical blade, King Arthur dubbed the young man on both shoulders. 'Stand up as a knight,' he said. 'Rise, Sir Percival.'

A great feast followed. Music and fanfare filled the hall. Knights, nobles, and royalty from all of Albion rejoiced together.

Sir Lancelot watched, pride swelling his heart. *Percy, a knight.* He shook his head in wonder. *Yet seldom has a man deserved the honour more.*

Next to Sir Lancelot, Lady Elayne beamed. Blessed with child, no expectant mother looked happier nor more radiant than she.

The festivities unfolded throughout the day. It was a jubilant occasion, mired only by the unsavoury behaviour of the Minstrels of Knoberton and, in particular, their chief player, Gaston le Grece, whose bawdy ballads made the hardiest knights blush.

At the height of merriment, King Arthur honoured his brave knights for their courage against the Saxon horde, but special praise was bestowed on Sir Gawain and Sir Lavaine for their part in rescuing Albion's queen. Yet, it was Sir Lancelot who was awarded the greatest honour. King Arthur requested the esteemed knight's presence atop the royal dais. 'You shall be king for the day!' he proclaimed grandly. 'Come, my friend, sit upon my throne.'

The revellers cheered gamely, and despite Sir Lancelot's protests, he was obliged to take the king's gilded seat beside Guinevere.

'The king's throne for a day,' the drunken Gaston bellowed, 'and perchance the king's bed for a night?' He raised his goblet toward the queen and winked.

Knights, lords, and ladies chortled with mirth, and so did the king, but neither Sir Lancelot nor Guinevere shared their enthusiasm. Nor did Sir Gawain, who watched with a deep frown creasing his noble brow. Nor Lady Elayne, who stared at the couple seated atop the dais with sadness.

~ The End ~

Begin the Timothy Williams Saga!

When Timothy's school becomes the subject of a demon takeover, he and his two friends, Rupert, and George, must unmask their foe. Timothy is forced into a battle for survival, not only in the real world but in his very dreams, where he must fight his nemesis to prevent Hell on Earth.

Blood-thirsty battles, monstrous demons, dodgy haircuts and enough possessed wildlife to fill a Satanic zoo!

'A full-on teenage adventure. Original, humorous, and highly imaginative. A rip-roaring read!' **BookViral**

Hell on Earth? Not if Timothy can help it.

Timothy Williams 3

Hellfire & Angel Light

Coming 2024!

After encountering a peculiar creature deep in the woods, Bennie and his friends are whisked away on a fantastical adventure that carries them to bizarre, far-flung places and exposes them to a terrifying enemy.

To rescue Christmas and the planet, Bennie and his friends must coax Earth's most reclusive hero from retirement.

Jump into the blue and join Bennie and his friends on a whirlwind adventure this Yuletide—a fun, festive story for all the family!

THE AUTHOR

Iestyn Long lives with his family in the historic village of Lavenham, in the Suffolk countryside. He is reasonably tall and narrow but desperately running out of hair, and although English, he has a Welsh name that is a constant confusion to one and all.

While listening to the tunes of Sir Cliff, Iestyn enjoys observing ants, stroking sparrows, drinking copious amounts of tea, and breathing—all of which he likes to practice on a regular basis.

Iestyn writes Young Adult fiction. Expect high-adventure, monstrous demons, epic battles, and dark humour.

For loads of extra demon-hunting stuff, visit these websites:
https://www.demon-hunter.co.uk
https://www.demonhuntersupplies.co.uk